The Luminous Planet

Hannah Klinge

The Luminous Planet

2023

© 2023 Hannah Klinge
Translated from Danish, *Den Lysende Planet* by
Sofie Hauch

Publisher: BoD – Books on Demand, Hellerup, Denmark
Press: BoD – Books on Demand, Norderstedt, Germany
ISBN: 978-87-4305-480-1

Preface

I wonder how many international resolutions have received the kind of attention that the 17 Development Goals have received. I'm referring to the seventeen goals for sustainable development adopted by the United Nations' General Assembly on 25 September 2015, formally known as: *R 70/1: Transforming our world*, and sometimes also called *Agenda 2030*.

All the members states' 193 heads of state and parliament voted in favour of the 17 Sustainable Development Goals. I don't know of any other resolution that has become the focus of so many presentations, talks, articles, conferences, seminars and webinars, decisions, books, courses – and now, and this is truly wonderful: artistic attention in the form of poetry, sculpture, art installations, essays, stories, songs, theatre, paintings, photos, and much else – and now: a fairy tale.

And it is truly a wonderful artistic effort we have been given with Hannah Klinge's *The Luminous Planet*. Bestselling Danish author Suzanne Brøgger wrote to me in an e-mail regarding Hannah and the book: "What a magical girl she is, and such an original, important book. It certainly deserves to be shared widely with the world, and in schools in particular." I was given permission to share Suzanne Brøgger's words, and I do so with great pleasure, because they encapsulate precisely and beautifully the significance of the book. *The Luminous Planet* is an original and important book, and right on point: the schools, the children, are so infinitely important in this context – as, indeed, in all contexts. And the deeply serious fact of the matter is precisely that we are talking about the world that our children are going to inhabit, that our children are going to inherit, the world that we are currently stewarding on their behalf. And as we so often say: We must hand on to our children a better world than the one we ourselves inherited. Easy words to say, but what do they mean? What does the word "better" mean in this regard? What kind of better world are we talking about? The Sustainable Development Goals and *The Luminous Planet* can tell us something about that. Indeed, that is what the goals and *The Luminous Planet* are all about, or – it is what they are also about. A better and different world.

What I found particularly remarkable about *The Luminous Planet* is that Hannah Klinge's narrative is integrally linked with the 17 Alignments *'transforming ourselves to transform the world'* which are concerned with the fact that our inner world, our thoughts, feelings, and ideas, create our outer reality. In order to contribute to the positive development of the world, we each therefore must examine our own inner development.

I send my very best wishes to Planet Earth and to *The Luminous Planet* on its onward journey. It has been an honour and a great delight to read and to be allowed to recommend the book in this manner.

Steen Hildebrandt
Professor emeritus, PhD
Frederiksberg, Denmark, July 1st, 2021

The Luminous Planet

1

The planet shone with such warmth that it humbly captured the full attention of its admirers. Somewhere in the universe it flourished and grew brighter day by day. It radiated a love so sincere that anyone immediately felt welcome simply at the sight of it.

Orion tilted his head back and peered dreamingly through the small round window in the ceiling. It was impossible for him to describe what he was seeing using mere words that always proved inadequate when he reached this point. "... *simply at the sight of it.*" Orion concluded his last sentence on the paper without feeling that it was complete. He sighed and got up from his chair at the desk, where he spent most of his time.

The old desk was placed at the centre of the room, surrounded by eighteen walls that together formed Orion's home in the shape of a star. Not that Orion had ever thought about this, because it was hard to get a general view of the house from the inside. He had never been out on the other side of the star's walls and knew only the truth he could see through the ceiling window.

What he saw, he had written countless, countless thoughts about. His books filled the room from floor to ceiling and would soon make it entirely impossible for Orion to see what was outside in the unknown, should he wish to. Yet, Orion couldn't find a single sentence in his many books that adequately described the luminous planet.

For as long as he could remember, he had been pondering the existence of this planet. The story of its past. If it had always been as bright as it was now, even before Orion's time.

The frustration of ignorance tormented him more and more as the days went by. Most of all, he longed to be able to answer the question he asked himself every day: Was there life on the luminous planet? What else could be the cause of such glittering colour and energy? Something definitely distinguished this planet from the other seventeen that Orion could also see through the window in his star.

One of them was large and in constant motion. One emitted light in colours of violet and crimson. Around another, a dark grey cloud circled, making it difficult to see if the planet itself was even there. One was incredibly small, and it was only occasionally that Orion was able to see it.

Each of these planets was unique but Orion knew one thing they all had in common: negativity. They radiated an emptiness and mysterious silence, as if they had been abandoned. They seemed bleak and Orion sensed a sadness about them.

He had written books and stories about all the planets. Seventeen volumes that each carefully described the individual planets. Together they formed a series demonstrating what the universe looked like and how it was interconnected, seen from Orion's point of view through the round window.

But his work was not yet complete, and it bothered him immensely. There was still one book that Orion never managed to finish. The book about the luminous planet, which all the other planets orbited.

It was time for Orion to complete the eighteenth volume. It was as if the universe increasingly urged him to finish the book. And he did not intend to let it down.

2

The future belongs to everyone. Although some claim that a few own it, this is untrue. The future hovers everywhere, forever, and is constantly transformed into present. Thus, future can never be grasped, and we might as well say that the future belongs to no one.

The future is known by being unknown. It is hard to size up, and often surprising.

This morning on a little star in the universe, the future's unknown face knocked on the door.

Orion jumped out of his chair, causing a storm of letters on the papers that slowly fell toward the floor.

Never before had he heard a sound from the outside. It repeated itself. A low knocking on the other side of Orion's walls. He couldn't hear exactly where the sound came from, but it was with a frightening certainty from the *outside*. Orion looked around the room where he had lived for so long. He knew every nook and cranny and knew where every book was placed. Not that there was any system in the many piles that formed an untidy wall around the centre of the star. And yet the many books now seemed to him like a systematically created border whose purpose it was to keep Orion trapped within. He felt a sudden urge to break through this wall of words – an urge he had never felt before.

Orion therefore did the only thing that at this moment seemed right to him. He grabbed one book after another and removed them from the path he was eagerly trying to make. As bricks that are broken apart and open the way for new possibilities, Orion had now created a clear path toward one of the star's corners.

He stood with his nose pressed against the wall as an unfamiliar thought was born in his mind: How could he have allowed himself to describe the planets of the universe as if it were the final truth, when he had never met them? Spoken with them or explored them? When the only thing he had done was to study them from this one perspective that was his own.

Now Orion could not think of anything more wrong than all the descriptive words he had written down in his books. The suddenly empty words that he had thought expressed the whole truth. He tried to imagine someone writing about Orion and his life on the star in the same way that he had written his books. He was certain that no living being was able to get near the truth at such a distance. It would simply be impossible to know Orion's detailed writings, his well-reflected thoughts, his life, and – most unthinkable – *his* perspective. All the things that described Orion. All the things that Orion had let himself express about the other planets without a second thought.

Decisively, and with a clear sense of doing the right thing, Orion picked up a stack of blank papers and his writing tools and stepped out of his safe, familiar home, into the universe.

In that moment, he stepped into a future that for the first time in Orion's life would be completely unpredictable and surprising. A future that, second by second, was followed by the present of an adventure. An adventure about the search for truth.

3

A quiet rustling of the wind through the fresh green leaves could be heard between the trees. Tall boughs that through long ages had patiently pushed closer to their source of life, the sun. Beneath them lived their smaller siblings, confident and respected despite their small size. Bright seedlings encountering the rays of the sun for the very first time. Flowers in unimaginable, impressive colours that painted the forest floor as a reflection of the rainbow in the sky. Shrubs carrying fruits with a sweetness that came as no surprise considering their exotic appearance.

This beautiful and eternally budding forest encircled a bright meadow that stretched over a hilltop. Like a sea of gold, the grain waved gently in the morning breeze. A few flowers glinted like stars in this field, showing the way towards the meadow's edge near the top of the hill. Up there, a large tree with a mighty crown stood as king over the peaceful landscape. The eye could not see what was on the other side of the tree. But it was tempting to go there, through the soft leaves calmly swaying back and forth in the breeze. The sun had just risen and cast a magical light over the entire meadow.

Everything about this place was so beautiful and comforting that one hardly dared to describe it with words. It would be like trying to draw the sun with a *piece of coal. All around this meadow resided a tranquillity and an energy that made anyone feel understood and made better. This place was created in love – there could be no doubt about that.*

Orion smiled at the words he had carefully chosen to put down on the paper. His eighteenth volume, about the luminous planet, was now begun, and he felt a great joy in anticipation of all the stories that would fill the now blank, but expectant pages. Orion folded up the sheet containing his description of the meadow and gently drew his hand over the heads of grain. They were soft and warm. He was filled with a sense of calm that encouraged him to pass through the bright meadow.

Step by step he moved closer to the tree on the hilltop that would welcome him with a heartfelt joy.

Orion placed a hand on the wide trunk of the magnificent tree and looked up at its dark green crown. He smiled at the tree with respect and admiration before he continued toward the unknown slope of the hill. There he stopped, gaping at the sight that greeted him.

In the valley behind the hill, life and energy flourished in a way that Orion had never before seen. It was entirely impossible for him to describe the many unfamiliar objects he saw, so he simply stood there gaping, for once unusually lost for words. There were so many things happening, and every moment Orion noticed something new. His curiosity led him closer to this strange, impressive place that he intensely desired to know better. On closer hand, Orion saw several enormous objects in different white shapes. Circles, triangles, rectangles, and shapes of five and six sides he noticed. They grew larger with every step he got closer to them. The hollow shapes were connected by winding paths of white stones.

Orion noticed something shimmering encircled by the white path. It was something smooth and mirror-bright that reflected the sun so perfectly that it looked as if a piece of the sun had fallen to the ground and shone from there. It was a lake with the clearest water, without a single ripple to disturb the glimmering peace of the lake. Between the white shapes, whose purpose was yet inscrutable to Orion, grew flowers of all the colours of the rainbow. Tall trees of different kinds stood as guardians of the peace of this place. Not that there appeared to be any need for guardians.

Under a particularly remarkable tree in the distant valley, Orion suddenly caught sight of something that at once overwhelmed him and made his heart race furiously. On a bench beneath the green canopy of leaves, a figure was sitting, which by its activity revealed the answer to one of Orion's most intensely pondered questions about the luminous planet – whether it contained life. This figure was a being. A living being. Orion stared at it, dumbstruck, filled with a heady combination of fear and euphoria. Who was this being? Despite the long distance between them, Orion sensed a warmth when he regarded the strange being. Suddenly, it stood up, and Orion's eyes followed it as it moved down the white path.

After a short while, it arrived at a circular square. Orion's heart rejoiced upon hearing the sound of hearty laughter and happy noises as the being reached the small square. On wooden tables and chairs sat several other beings. In his excitement and bursting with curiosity, he went closer to the valley.

Near the square where several of the beings were assembled, a large, white, noiseless object suddenly appeared. It contained more of the beings, which now seemed to be leaving the vehicle that had brought them. Without so much as a whisper the large, white object quickly departed again, heading toward a place further away.

Orion squinted into the distance again and noticed fields, and rows of tree trunks forming long walls that sheltered smaller plants growing against them. It looked like edible plants, judging from their colourful fruits in orange, green, red, and purple shades.

Orion's thoughts were interrupted by a light breeze that caused a distant rushing sound. He looked toward the sudden sound only to discover a forest of towering, peculiar moving trees. They were all white and each had three long branches that rotated at the same speed in the wind. Orion had never seen anything like it.

He shook his head and expected to see these odd trees change colour to the natural green, but no. White, rotating treetops.

This was without doubt a mysterious place, unlike anything Orion knew from his little star. Yet, he had no intention of turning around. He wasn't sure what he had expected when he set out, but certainly not this. He had had no idea that the beautiful, luminous planet would also contain so many details. Perhaps he had just expected to arrive at a sphere of light. A globe of warmth. A loving radiance, smiling and gleaming, as he knew it from his window in the star. Never had he imagined that the luminous planet would be filled with so many unique creations. So much beauty for the eye that it was impossible to take it all in at once.

Although all these details only fuelled Orion's curiosity about the planet's story, he deliberately kept his distance from the valley.

Because for so long he had been observing this planet from afar. So many times had he wondered about it. Imagined and tried to guess what it might be. What it contained. But always from a viewpoint far away from it. Now he had zoomed in and dived right into the very thing his eyes had until now only seen across a great distance. Orion tilted his head back and tried in vain to see his comfortable home in the skies. For a brief moment he wanted nothing more than to return to his old, familiar perspective.

But the gentle breeze surrounding him wanted something else and it now softly swept Orion down into the planet's little valley, the luminous centre of the planet.

4

"Are you alive too?" Orion asked.

By a beautiful tree with flaming red leaves, a being sat with its back leaned against the trunk of the tree. A being, calm and with a dreaming look in the large, dark brown eyes. Eyes that now dwelt on Orion's small figure with wonder and curiosity.

"That depends on who you ask. If you ask the clock that stopped, it will certainly answer that I am alive. If you ask never-ending time itself, it will probably answer that my short lifespan is not even worth counting. But since you ask me, I, from my point of view, will answer yes. A heartfelt yes!"

Orion again stood speechless while he tried to search his mind for the right words. He was really speaking to one of the planet's living beings.

"Are there others like you on this planet?" Orion finally asked.

The being gave a warm laugh and gently picked one of the many red flowers that formed a living mat under their feet.

"There is no other flower like this one. It is entirely unique and possesses its own story. However, it has a whole field of brothers and sisters that look just like it and partly are like to it. But this beautiful red flower is definitely its own." He smiled at Orion before continuing: "I would guess that you haven't been here

23

very long. Come, sit here under the tree. I want to tell you about this red flower, which is simply one shade in the colourful story of the planet where you are right now – and which you are so curious about." Orion carefully sat down and leaned against the tree under the umbrella of leaves that looked so much like wisps of fire. He breathed deeply of the fresh air.

"I want to know if your planet was always as luminous as it is now. It is not like the other planets. It is full of unique details, but I cannot figure out if it was always so. It is like a radiant centre, but I cannot see why."

The being with the loving eyes replied: "I understand your wondering about that. In short, I can tell you that this planet of life and joy was not always as flourishing as it is now. Just like everything else, it has passed through its own development. Begun as a humble seed and grown into a mighty and complex tree. Growing it will be always. But the story of this place is long, and you cannot receive the whole truth from a single mouth."

Orion interrupted the being, eager to know more: "Please, just tell me what you know. About your story."

The being laughed again, impressed by the stranger's curiosity. He himself was just as curious to know more about the stranger's story and origin, but he sensed that he would not get a single answer to his questions until he had told the stranger about his own past. He cleared his throat before beginning: "Well, my story you shall have. First my name you shall learn. I am Terra. My name comes from a place far, far from here. A place that hardly exists anymore."

5

A loud crash sounded on the other side of the wooden walls of the house. The impact shook the little table, making the hot tea splash and burn Terra's small fingers. He winced and glared with reproach out of the window. Dark clouds glided over the forest as a warning of catastrophe. The forest that shrank with every passing second. The little saplings could not keep up with the efficiency of the sharp knives and were forced constantly to whisper goodbye to their elder siblings.

"Get more wood!" a deep voice shouted through the door, and a muscled arm pointed at the fire that had nearly gone to sleep and no longer performed its duty – to keep the little hut warm.

Terra got up and was met on the other side of the door by a merciless cold. He looked down at the large pieces of wood lying beside the old axe. How he hated this task. When the blade split the wood in two, he heard a cry of pain that rent his ears. *Murderer*, he thought.

Emptyhanded, he returned to the hut and put on one more jumper.

"I painted it when I was about your age. Look at all the green colours. I can barely recall that sight anymore." The old woman sighed and gave the painting to her grandson, the thoughtful and now young man.

He looked at the painting with a dreaming look in his eyes. A planet seen from a distant point of view, with great trees covering the entire surface. Leaves in every shade of green created a positive energy around the planet. An untouched and flourishing forest, a blossoming of life on land.

"What is going to become of us?" Terra asked, before he continued, despairing: "Each day more and more of us fall, just as the trees did. Soon it will be so empty here that no soul can survive, or rather, *will* survive in this place. This world of grey and foggy shadows kills the joy in me. I cannot help but blame myself for not doing more to prevent it. I could have stopped him. Perhaps all of them. I could have told him what I saw in the future. I could have kept some seeds and sown them now, so we could replant the forest again. I wish I had done something, anything to save our people. Anything to prevent this ruin."

The old woman looked at him with love, her eyes full of sorrow. "Terra, your father's actions are not yours. Shame that he was part of cutting down the forest is not for you to bear. You cannot hold his ignorance against him, but forgive and try to understand him. He believed that the only chance of his and your survival was to obey the selfish commands of others. Certainly, he was one of those who killed the forest, but not out of an evil mind."

She went to the dresser that stood in the corner of the little room, opened the bottom drawer, and carefully took out a small wooden box. On the top was painted in bright green a tree on the ground and three birds in flight.

"How beautiful it is," Terra said when his grandmother sat down next to him on the bed.

"A beautiful exterior, but an even more beautiful interior," she replied.

"May I open it?" Terra asked curiously.

She smiled at him, stroking his hair. "For that you'll need a key."

He looked at her, questioning, and she explained: "In this box are 15 seeds, children of different kinds of flowers, plants, and trees. It has been passed down in the family through many generations. Our ancestors created it to ensure that our planet would be forever fertile and flourishing. To ensure that it would not end up barren, arid, and empty like now."

Terra sprang up. "Then let us sow these seeds as soon as possible. I know a spot of soil on the other side of the cemetery that is not completely dried out."

"Sit down, sweetheart." Her voice was serious. "Once lightning has struck the treetop and split it into a thousand pieces, it will never grow again. Terra, these seeds in the box have no future on this planet. This planet will, as you said, soon be entirely empty. *Deathly* empty."

She handed over the box to this good soul whose brown eyes were full of tears. He knew what she was going to ask of him. He wiped away the tears before whispering: "The key only exists in the place where the seeds' future resides. I have to leave."

He said the final word hoping that he had misunderstood her. But he could see in her wise eyes that he had understood exactly what she had in mind.

She pointed to another of her paintings that hung on the wall in the centre of all the others. Terra had never noticed it before, which was odd because it shone with beauty and immediately captured Terra's full attention. The painting showed a night sky with hundreds of stars. In the middle, a bright green round leaf floated. It looked like a planet, but it was unfamiliar to Terra.

"Yes, Terra, you must journey to that place whose future is bright and flourishing. Full of hope and possibilities. There is no right way to go there, nor a wrong one. There is only your way. Follow the path your soul shows you and walk it to the end. Then you will find the key you seek. The key to the seeds in the box, to the seedlings of the future."

Terra was moved to tears again as he stood looking up at the enormous and beautiful tree in front of him. It felt like being reunited with an old friend, although the tree, like everything else in this place, was unfamiliar to him. The tree budded with hope, confirming Terra's belief that his mission was possible here.

He looked around but did not need long before he had decided where to begin. Where he would create and build new life, new hope in the form of a burgeoning forest, thriving fields, and luscious plants.

His mind made up, he walked down towards the valley, impressed by its magnificence. He imagined all the life that this place would accommodate perfectly. When he arrived in the valley and stood surrounded by the cradling hills, his thoughts went to the little seed box.

"The key only exists in the place where the seeds' future resides," he repeated to himself.

He closed his eyes and saw in his mind's eye a path that extended further with every step he took. On his journey here, he had followed this path the whole way to his arrival on this planet. Despite not knowing the way, nor the destination, Terra had trusted that this path that he saw in front of him would lead him to the right place. Every step was important, also when it occasionally led him on a detour or into suffering. Because without the detours, the dead ends, and the delays, he would never had reached this destination, which had become his goal. Each step led him on the way.

Terra suddenly noticed something shining at the end of the path in his mind. He followed it, eyes closed, until he felt a powerful light shining on his face. He opened his eyes and saw that the light came from the ground. It was a tiny lake that reflected the sunlight so perfectly that Terra had to squint to be able to focus on the surface. And below the mirror-bright surface, a small object, also glinting in the sunlight, caught his attention. He carefully reached into the icy water and gasped when he saw what he had just picked up. Bright gold covered the form of a heavy, long-sought key.

6

Under the red tree, Orion was looking at Terra, impressed. For the moment, the joy of receiving was alive in Orion. He deliberately kept quiet, because any word uttered would upset the balance of the story and topple it. Just now it stood, beautiful as it was, requiring no additions, questions, or further remarks.

Terra stood up and peered down through the valley. He had caught sight of something, because now he motioned with his wooden staff as if waving at somebody.

"Come along, my friend," he said to Orion.

Together, they walked across the field of beautiful red flowers. They headed up a small hill, and Orion was curious to know what was on the other side of it. He could no longer hold back his questions.

"Where are we going?" he asked.

"Now I recognise you again!" Terra said, laughing. "Together we are heading to the planet's luminous centre."

At the crest of the hill, Terra suddenly stopped. "Wait here." He tilted his head to one side and peered keenly at Orion, scrutinising him. Then he nodded to himself. "So, you finally found us." He walked on ahead, leaving Orion behind in wonder.

Orion expected Terra to return, so he sat down to wait. He looked up at the sky that was so simple when it was only painted in one colour. He let out a sign and thought about Terra's story, which unlike the blue sky had been all but simple. So Terra also, like Orion himself, had left his home and journeyed to this planet. But unlike Orion, he had left a place that eventually had become so ruined by catastrophes that the journey here was his only chance for survival.

An icy-blue cloud appeared in the peaceful sky and interrupted Orion's musings. Its shadow covered Orion like a veil, and he shivered from the sudden chill. In that moment, he noticed a figure in the field further down the hillside. Orion's eyes widened. The figure moved steadily up the hill, and before long Orion would make another encounter with a being from the luminous planet. This being was darker in hue and more powerfully built than Terra. It approached Orion at a relaxed pace and brought a warm energy with it. The being soon reached the crest of the hill and met Orion with a broad smile, clearly pleased to meet the small being that Terra had just told about.

"Welcome, Orion," the being said in a strong voice.

Orion wondered briefly. Perhaps this being had arrived in the same way as Terra? "Have you always lived here?" he asked.

The being peered curiously at Orion. "*Always* is a very long time. I wonder if there is anything that is longer than always. Can you double always? And can you split always into smaller parts, as we so often do? Perhaps always is one continuum that can never be split or doubled, but only exists as a whole that is forever everywhere. Perhaps always is a description of time being one." The being fell silent. The cloud and its shadow disappeared and the warmth from the sun could be felt again.

"Who are you?" Orion asked after a pause, hoping for a more comprehensible answer.

"My name is Pheko. But listen, little one. If you really want to know who I am, you must hear a tale whose words shed light on my past in the most truthfull way."

Pheko took the final step to the top of the hill and sat down next to Orion. Orion, who in his abundant curiosity regarded Pheko impatiently and asked him to tell the tale at once. Pheko cleared his throat before beginning to speak in his powerful voice.

"Once upon a time there was a mountain, which was the mightiest of all. It was so high that its peak reached far into the clouds, and it was so wide that no living thing could pass all the way around it within a lifetime. It stood tall and beautiful and took good care of all the life that inhabited its sides. In summer, the mountain was painted with colourful flowers, and in winter with glittering snow. All the flowers and all the snowflakes lived in mutual respect in the belief that they were all equally valuable and therefore deserved the same value in life.

"It was a winter's night upon the mighty mountain. 1 snowflake, small and beautiful, had just landed on the soft snow covering the highest mountain peak. The snowflake looked down over the wonderful mountainside that glittered and shone in the starlight. It was a breathtaking sight. There was so much snow that the little snowflake was filled with an exhilarating feeling of never getting tired of wanting to see more. To have more. Suddenly, it had an idea. It rocked forward a little and grabbed hold of the other snowflakes surrounding it. The other snowflakes complained, as they were now attached to the snowflake, who had grown slightly bigger by this manoeuvre. The snowflake laughed, deeply enjoying the feeling. It rolled forward again, growing larger and larger. The little snowflakes that contributed to its gain in size lost their own value in the process, but the snowflake had to regard for this. It had a goal: It must grow bigger.

"When the rays of the morning sun peered around the side of the mountain, the snowflake was no longer a snowflake. It had become a snowball. The snowball rolled at full speed down the mountainside, because there was so much snow to take from. It rolled cheerfully down the white slope where harmony and peace resided. A group of snowflakes lay here in the quiet of the morning, and suddenly caught sight of a huge ball accelerating towards them at high speed. They saw how the snowflakes on the higher slopes lost their worth as they were absorbed into the big ball. And within seconds, this became their own fate. They were no longer the same snowflakes they had been before. And the big ball was not the same either. It was richer than ever before.

"In its frenzy it continued faster and further down the mountain, its focus fixed on the way ahead. It no longer heard the many screams and complaints. It no longer saw the individual snowflakes losing their worth. It saw only its goal.

"As the snowball grew larger, it also became more and more selfish and greedy. And it had now grown so heavy that it not only raked in the white snow. The soil, that in summer fed the many flowers, was also taken into the ball, which became soiled and dirty.

But the worst part was the dreadful trail of devastation that it left behind on the mountainside; where the ball had rolled, none of the winter's snow remained. And near the trail the surrounding snowflakes had become so poor and deprived that they could no longer see any meaning in life. Not a single flower would be able to grow here for many summers to come, the way the soil had been torn up and the protective cover of snow had been destroyed.

"This poverty had caused an enormous inequality and imbalance on the mountain. It was as if the dark, heavy ball made the mountain start to tip. This could not last. And indeed, it did not.

"It was the third night. The ball had grown vast, impossibly heavy, and grossly rich on snowflakes and soil. In its blinding greed of constantly wanting more it entirely failed to see the large jagged rock that stood at the bottom of the mighty mountain, waiting to confront the injustice. All the ball saw was the pure white snow covering the surface of the rock, and it accelerated further. At the very moment it was at its largest, fastest, and most blinded by greed, the ball smashed into the solid rock. A gigantic crash sounded and shook the mighty mountain. The ball was shattered into thousands of pieces and disintegrated in an instant into a cloud of brown and white atoms. Time stood still. The ball, formerly so rich, which had ruined so much on its way, had lost. It could only lose. Because no place dominated by selfishness and greed could persist.

"The countless snowflakes and the enormous amounts of soil hung suspended in the air, sighed with relief, liberated from the poverty in which they had been trapped. In a moment of absolute silence, one snowflake moved off in a new direction; it glided slowly towards a future where it would fight to ensure that the injustice of poverty would never exist."

9

Pheko's powerful gaze met Orion's as he brought his tale to a close. In that moment, Orion realised that Pheko was one of the many snowflakes whose life had lost value because of the greedy snowball. Whose life had been forced into unjust poverty. And Orion could not bear this thought. A tear fell to the ground as he said with great sadness: "It is hard for me to understand how you have lived through such a cata-strophe. Forced into the unjust nature of poverty and seen your brothers and sisters fall. Left your home forever. And yet, you are smiling. I struggle to fathom how your soul can carry on living at all after so much injustice. Tell me if it is just an appearance, and if deep down you are filled with a constant sadness that you have learned to live with and hide? Is it even possible to feel genuine joy after such a tremendous disaster?"

Pheko sat down by Orion's side. He brushed the tears from his cheek and asked: "Tell me, is it possible for you to smile after shedding a tear?"

He continued, as Orion at once broke into a smile at this question: "The misery of poverty that over-came my planet I'll never forget. The sorrow will never depart from my memory. Nor will my brothers and sisters who fell prey to the injustice of poverty ever leave my heart. It all lives within me in its own way. But simply because it continues to live in me does not mean that I have to live *by* it. That I have to let the sorrow and misery fill me up and thus govern me. Inside me there will always be room for joy. Our inner self is not simple. We are not either happy or sad. We contain sorrow and joy, happiness and unhappiness, good and evil. But it is simple that we can choose what to focus on.

"I believe that the great frustration and grief that the catastrophe on my former planet caused me created an equal amount of gratitude and joy within me. When all was at its darkest, I realised the need for light. When all was full of misery, a desire to fight for joy grew within me. When injustice reigned, I at once knew the necessity of justice.

"So in answer to your question: Yes, a sadness does live in me after the unjust catastrophe that happened to me and the people of my planet. A sadness that I have not learned to hide, but instead learned to use to show me happiness. I use it as a tool to remind me of the necessity of fighting so that no one else will ever have to experience what I did.

"By accepting the grief of my past and choosing to focus on the present and the joy of the future, a genuine happiness lives within me."

Orion smiled up at Pheko. The tale had a happy ending.

Suddenly something wet struck Orion's forehead. He looked up at the sky, which had changed into a heavy grey blanket. Another drop fell on him.

"What's going on?" Orion exclaimed, bewildered.

Pheko looked with puzzlement at Orion, who did not appear to have experienced rain before. I do wonder where he comes from, he thought to himself. Pheko refrained from asking because he was sure that the right moment would come when Orion himself was ready to tell about his origins. And it was certainly not this moment, because now the little being had got up and was dashing back and forth trying to avoid being hit by the raindrops.

"Do not worry, little one. Come with me – I know a place where we can find shelter from the rain."

They were nearing the edge of the field and could continue their walk sheltered beneath the rich green canopy of the great trees. A brook ran beside them, babbling in time with their steps. They walked along in silence, listening to nature's voice singing so beautifully. Suddenly another voice rang out that Orion had not heard before. He could not see where it came from and increased his pace in order to find out. Soon Pheko was lagging behind and called to Orion:

"Just go ahead, I'll meet you later, little one."

Orion briefly glanced over his shoulder and saw Pheko turning aside in another direction. The singing voice sounded louder and louder, and Orion

41

curiously followed it. He went to the brook and walked along it for another while until he caught sight of what he was seeking: the being to whom the voice belonged.

It was sitting on a small bridge that connected the brook's two banks. It had long hair that fell down over a translucent light blue dress that enveloped the being's delicate figure.

Now Orion clearly heard the words of the song that enchanted him by the beautiful voice.

"Bridge over troubled water, I will ease your mind. Like a bridge over ..."

The being looked up with a dreaming look in its eyes and caught sight of Orion.

"You were in my dream last night," the being said in a sweet voice. It looked at Orion as if examining him closely, then stood up and placed a warm hand on his cheek.

"Orion. You have come from far away. Thank you for the open mind you bring, your searching to know more. It is admired."

The being laughed at Orion's gaping expression.

"I confuse you, don't I? My name is Agua."

His curiosity getting the better of him again, Orion burst in and began to ask if she had always lived on this planet or if she, like Terra and Pheko, had also fled from a catastrophe-filled place, what her past looked like, and, besides, how she could have dreamed about him. He did not manage to ask any more, because Agua raised a finger to her lips, gesturing for him to be silent. She said in a calm voice:

"Dear Orion, do not ask, but listen. I know why you are here. You note down thoughts and experiences in words, thereby perpetuating know-ledge, among other things. Perhaps you are not yourself aware of it, but your visit to our planet is absolutely crucial. An important understanding of life awaits you here. Awaits being found and communicated. For there are others than you in this universe who must know about the evolution of this planet. About the past and insights of its inhabitants, about the development of the future. About how darkness can be transformed into light. Do not think that your journey to this place was simply an action based on a random idea. It was an action based on an important step towards approaching the truth. A striving to enlighten the universe about goals that were attained in cooperation.

"I shall tell you my story, which is part of the truth of this luminous planet. I know that you possess the ability to listen, because I can see it in your eyes."

And Orion listened. He listened to Agua's wise words, her gentle voice, and the story in her eyes. Side by side they crossed over the little bridge and stepped into a tale about a heart's endless thirst.

10

Agua looked down at the blank sheet of paper in her lap. The scorching wind was like a desperate whisper imploring her to choose her words with care. She took a deep breath and prayed that The Powerful One would understand the people's desperate situation with this letter. She began to write.

In a future not far off, we will no longer be able to exist our planet. Drought and lack of water will dominate and kill all living things. The competition for the planet's water is growing. The conflict is spreading everywhere and sows strife between friends. Splits up families. Digs deeper trenches between strangers.

You must realise that the amount of water is scarce. At the same time, poison is being poured into our rivers and pollutes the limited amount of clean water we have left as if it were an endless resource. The pollution causes countless diseases, especially in this time of heatwaves. The number of migrants who are forced to leave their place of birth to search for clean water is steadily rising. But not only that, more and more people die from diseases and drought.

We are concerned about your lack of action in solving this growing problem. It is your ruthless drilling of deep wells and excessive use of the planet's clean water that has produced these serious consequences.

If the problem is not solved immediately, we will all be forced to flee for our survival. But here we already encounter the next problem: Whereto, when the entire planet will soon suffer drought?

I beg you to realise that the lack of water is life-threatening, and to fight with us to save our planet!

- Agua

She ran through the dusty town, hoping to deliver the letter to The Powerful One in time. She knew that every second without action would double the problem. She wanted to explain to him that there was only one thing to do: They must protect and re-establish the lakes and rivers and any other water bodies that could still be saved.

Agua's thoughts were interrupted by a sudden scream a little further ahead of her. She sped up and saw what had caused the shrill voice to cry out.

Their last waterhole, the pool that kept them all alive, had turned a dark green colour. Silver-grey clots covered the surface of the water, and the now poisoned water gave off a repulsive stench. It must be poisoned. Because in one end of the waterhole floated a small child's body. Its face was pale and the lips green-tinged. The child was dead.

A heart-wrenching sob sounded from the child's mother as she rushed toward the little body. Agua ran after her and at the last moment managed to get hold of her arm before she also touched the poisoned water.

"I only sent him out to fetch water. I didn't know it was poisoned too. I sent him out."

She cried with a pain that became more and more unbearable to herself and those standing by, staring.

"I sent him out," she kept saying over and over. Agua had to use all her strength to hold her back, until the mother finally gave up and collapsed on the ground.

"It is The Powerful One's fault. He killed my son. He ignores our problem and lets the water disappear through our fingers," she shouted angrily.

Agua sat down beside her, gently stroking the crying mother's hair, while she cast around in her mind trying to remember where the next waterhole was located. There was not one nearby. As long as the poisoned pool fumed in the heat, it was not safe to remain here. They had to flee.

Agua's heavy legs begged for a break. The group had walked through the dust for so long that they had lost all sense of time and place. Agua ignored the sickening thirst and the complaints of the people and carried on walking. Suddenly an image appeared in Agua's worried mind. She closed her eyes and saw a huge ocean in front of her. The water resembled liquid gold that glimmered harmoniously in time with the waves. Agua stood high above and looked down over the endless sea. Above her, white clouds sailed, as if embracing the sea and protecting it. Protected it from dangers and thieves. Agua felt herself as a part of the cloud, as if she were one with it. She had a sense that she was the protector of the sea and felt a strong sudden desire to realise this vision.

A dust cloud swept past, recalling Agua from her vision. She looked back at the people wandering behind her through the dirty streets. Their eyes were full of fear, their hearts full of sorrow. A deathly silence held sway among them. Agua looked up at the sky with concern, where a storm was brewing. She tried to remember how long they had been walking. It had been a long time since they left the poisoned pool. Many had fallen since then.

They had not seen any sign of water yet, so Agua had decided that they would have to go and face their greatest enemy, The Powerful One, who possessed their final hope: the well. The Powerful One had dug countless wells to secure enough water to supply his own need and greed. Agua's plan was to break into the wellhouse and confront The Powerful One, whose selfishness would otherwise defeat all the planet's people. But the problem was that the people became weaker and fewer with every passing moment. The people she saw behind her had abandoned hope. Their eyes were empty, and they would soon accept the harsh consequence of thirst.

They followed their leader, but increasingly doubted her hopeful words. They no longer reacted when someone gave in to the pain of thirst and fell down in the dusty street.

"Fight!" Agua kept shouting to encourage the flock behind her. Perhaps she was mostly shouting at that part of herself that also felt like giving up. She took one more step.

On the horizon she now saw The Powerful One's blue gates and commanded herself to carry this fight to the end. She increased her pace and purposefully moved ahead.

Finally, she reached the enormous gates. There were 6 gates in total. They were arranged like six points in the wall that formed a large circle. A white drop was painted on one gate that was a lighter blue colour than the rest. The well must be on the other side of it. Agua listened. Why was it so quiet? A chill swept over her as she sensed something was wrong. Quickly she spun around and let out a gasp at the sight that met her. There was not a single person behind her. Squinting, she saw instead the many bodies lying motionless along the road toward the gates. Everyone had fallen.

Agua caught sight of the body that had fallen closest to her. At once, she knew who it was. Because the body was crouched forward in the same way that it had been when it had lost its child in the poisoned pool. This mother had followed Agua so far but did not manage to reach the goal with her. Agua sat down beside her and slowly caressed the dusty hair. Anger and despair grew within her. She closed her eyes but could not hold back the tears. She opened her eyes again, now seeing the world through the water of sorrow. Everything looked wet, as if it were under the sea.

A loud creaking sounded from the gates and reminded Agua that everything was anything but wet. Suddenly the gate with the white drop began to open slowly and Agua knew that she had to go inside.

On the other side of the gate and the walls, Agua could see that they did not form a circle but the shape of a large drop. And in the middle was a well. Agua ran over and peered into it. It was so deep that she could not see the bottom. She picked up a large rock and dropped it down the well to get an idea of how deep it was. There was a long silence, and Agua did not think she heard any hard bumps. Instead, she suddenly heard a deep voice emit a scream before silence fell once more.

"The Powerful One!" Agua thought. He must have fallen into the well as he was trying to get more water. Now a painful thirst struck Agua forcefully, and she was unable to think clearly anymore. She used her last remaining strength to draw the bucket out of the well, hoping intensely to find water in it. Her jaw dropped. The bucket was full of clean water.

11

"What did you do with the water?" Orion asked when Agua had finished speaking.

"I created a spring. But not on the planet where the water came from, because all hope for the soil there had dried up. I sought out a place where clean water could flow for the benefit of all. A place where the water would not dry up. I wanted to do everything in my power to avoid the death of water forever. Because I had seen the danger of ignoring the problem. Seen the catastrophe that had ensued. And I knew that the only right thing I could do was to turn the last hope into reality. I must bring the last of the water to a safe place and turn it into a spring. A spring whose water would forever trickle with life and ensure life.

"So I came to this place. And here I achieved my goal. In the stream we are now walking along runs the water from the bucket that I brought with me. It was the last hope but it never died because I let it flow within me until the end. And now it will forever flow from the spring."

Orion looked at the small, delicate being who possessed so much strength. He was nearly convinced that all beings must possess this strength.

"Dear Orion, thank you for listening. Come, I want to show you our luminous centre," Agua said and led

Orion toward the place he had wanted to experience for so long. Until now he had been led around the luminous centre, but he had by no means forgotten about its presence. Now the time had finally come to enter it. He took a deep breath before he moved closer to the light. Closer to the truth.

12

The planet's centre was only more impressive that what it had seemed to be from a distance.

It was joy turned into a place. It was as if everything had its place and belonged.

Agua led the way to the beginning of the white path that wound around the outskirts of the city. Following the path was a unique experience, because with every step leading one along the path and on toward the centre, the more free one felt. Around the path grew beautiful, healthy flowers that with their colours offered one a warm welcome. Along the path, one passed many large white objects that aroused in one a curiosity to step inside them. Great trees could be seen everywhere, creating a sense of shelter so pleasant that one at once felt at home.

Agua moved lightly over the white stones, like a drop flowing securely in the stream. Soon the drop joined a larger fellowship in the form of a radiant lake.

It shone at once so beautifully and brightly that the eyes were drawn to it but almost couldn't look at it directly. Surrounding the lake, a frame of fresh green plants grew, encircling the luminous centre with hope.

For long periods one could daydream before the almost magical lake, by which one felt purified simply by looking at it. However, dream and reality are not always combined, but interrupt each other with their differences. Here the dream was suddenly interrupted by a real voice speaking real facts. The voice said that this lake expanded as one's dreams grew.

This bright voice belonged to a very small being with large eyes and an eager joyful disposition that one noticed immediately. Chunlian was her name.

Chunlian gestured to continue along the white path. She stopped by a small bench that leaned against one of the large white objects with square windows. Chunlian sat down on the bench and began to tell a story:

Inside the large white object she learned everything she desired to learn and everything that she had never known it was possible to learn. But it had not always been so.

She came from a planet where learning had been forbidden. Not for all, but for Chunlian. She was one of many who from birth had been forbidden the key to learning: symbols of learning. It was necessary to master the symbols of learning in order to understand knowledge. Because knowledge was written using these signs and thus only accessible to those who understood them. Of course, knowledge could be shared by word of mouth so it would be available to all, but it had become illegal to do so and therefore impossible. "There is a reason why some are ignorant," it was explained. So if one was deemed ignorant, one was relegated to a life without permissible development.

But those who did master the symbols of learning did not share equal status either. The knowing ones, as they were called, were divided into cells depending on how many symbols of learning they knew. In these cells they gave all the time they had until it was entirely spent. When this moment arrived, they were expected to master the complete system of symbols of learning, or they would be deemed ignorant too. The long time that the knowing ones spent in the cells revolved around acquiring a system that would at some later time make knowledge accessible to them. Not acquiring knowledge that would be useful immediately. "They need to learn to learn."

A few were more proficient at the symbols of learning than others, which resulted in better status points. The more status points, the better status and the better cells and treatment they would receive from the wise one.

The wise one was the one who knew most and was thus regarded as the wisest in every cell. The wise one possessed powers that it could use as it desired. First of all, it possessed the time of the knowing ones and could fill it with words about the symbols of learning that every wise one was passionately committed to. Secondly, it possessed the right to treat the knowing ones in the way that the wise one deemed necessary, whether the knowing ones liked it or not. Thirdly, the wise one possessed the power to decide the knowing ones' wellbeing and future. Because the actions, words, and awarded status points of the wise one had a decisive impact on the future wellbeing and development of each knowing one. In other words, the wise ones held each knowing one's future in their hands. "This is called fairness."

The whole system was structured in a way that seemed anything but optimal for the development of the knowing ones, although this was supposedly its purpose. They had to give all their time to a wise one, who was forced to follow the framework of the system, not the knowing ones, whether the wise one wanted to or not. They must accept only learning about the symbols of learning, which would only become useful after the long time in the cell was over. And they must put their life in the hands of another, who all too often formed it in a negative way.

Chunlian, who had been deemed ignorant before birth, was eager to gain access to knowledge. So she often hid behind the cell doors and tried to learn the symbols of learning though the door cracks. But she only picked up limited fragments of learning.

She wondered if the knowing ones inside the cell also only learned limited amounts. Because through the cracks Chunlian heard a monotonous voice that droned on endlessly and without making much sense. Chunlian could see the knowing ones sitting nearly motionless in long rows. She discovered that they were locked in place by chains, which only the wise one could decide when to release. Meanwhile, one of their hands moved constantly, writing down every word coming from the wise one's mouth. Occasionally, the wise one would ask a question, release the chains, and the knowing ones would urgently leaf through their papers until they found the answer that the wise one was looking for. Status points were awarded. Thus it continued in the same fashion until the knowing ones had donated so much time to the wise one that they began to feel poor on time themselves. In exchange they had learned the symbols of learning, and those who had any strength left would go on to use them to understand some self-chosen knowledge. But it was far from all who were able to do this once their cell time was completed.

Once when Chunlian was peering through the door crack into a cell, she was shocked in a way she would never forget. This cell was one that she had followed from the beginning, when the knowing ones' eyes had been filled with energy and curiosity. They had been excited to learn the necessary symbols of learning and were eager to understand every word the wise one said. After some time, this joy had disappeared, but Chunlian thought that they were probably just tired from the hard work that the cell time implied.

But the third time Chunlian looked through the crack into the cell, the sight she encountered still frightens her whenever she thinks of it. The knowing ones sat in their rows as always, but the atmosphere in the cell was like never before. Some sat with their eyes closed. The heads of some hung down so heavily that if it had not been for the chains, they would fall forward onto the floor. Some sat with despair in their eyes and tears running down their cheeks. Some discussed angrily if they really had to give all their time to this meaningless cell. Some flailed their arms and legs in frustration as if trying to get away. Some were constantly writing notes, although their fingers were bleeding. Some sat with a crazy look in their eyes, whispering snide words at those who appeared to be unaffected by the situation. All the while the wise one spoke non-stop in the monotonous voice: "The necessary symbols of learning ..."

Chunlian gasped and pulled away from the cell door. She had never seen anything like this. She peered through the other doors. The same disastrous scenario. This cell time could not possibly affect their planet positively. Did the cell time really exist in order to develop the knowing ones as individuals? To prepare them for their future life? Did the system really exist for the benefit of the knowing ones, and, if not, for whom? Was there perhaps a higher power that benefited from the effect that the cell time had on the knowing ones and desired things to remain like this?

Chunlian was filled with despair and concern for her planet. She wanted to change the system of the cell time, but she suddenly wondered if change was even legal. She could not remember ever hearing about *developing, changing, or improving the system. Was there a reason for this?*

Chunlian was so worried about the knowing ones, and even the wise ones, who were also forced to follow the rules of the system. Because although the knowing ones and the wise ones were unhappy with the cell time, they ultimately accepted it. But Chunlian saw the serious impact it had on the planet: its beings did not learn how to handle their own or the planet's problems. They constantly created more and more problems, and it had long since become impossible to get a grasp of how all the problems were to be solved.

If nobody else intended to do anything about the system, Chunlian would do it herself. Because she knew one thing: A catastrophe must not be ignored or accepted. She had to act immediately.

Her action did not lead to a battle against the ignorant ones, the knowing ones, or the wise ones, but a battle against the system that had created these divisions.

Chunlian soon realised that in order to achieve what was supposedly the aim of the cell time – the acquisition of knowledge, understanding of the surrounding world, each individual's own insights, and thus development – a completely different system would have to be established. Nothing in the cell time system contributed to these 4 aims, and in fact in most cases did the opposite. Rethinking was necessary.

Therefore, she left her planet to find a place that could contain the learning system she believed was ideal. She did not journey long, because the place she was looking for did not demand a lot. Only that it would accept ongoing improvement and development and value understanding of the users of the system. Chunlian had travelled to the luminous planet where development was already underway.

She erected this place of learning for all those who desired to learn. The rooms inside were adapted to the type of learning taking place within them. Whether it was learning about nature, the history of the planet, ideas, art, care, or something else, the shape of the room, its size, and location were suited to the purpose. And learning might also take place outdoors when desired.

Those who undertook the teaching also adapted to those receiving teaching. They adjusted the difficulty, the needs, and the range of interests. Everything fell into a balance between the one who taught and the one who learned. This place of learning was built on the ideas of knowledge, understanding, realisation, and development. Four inseparable and interdependent concepts.

Chunlian related the final words with a deep joy and pride. She repeated that she was now teaching and learning everything she had ever wanted to learn and everything that she had never known it was possible to learn. And this learning, combined with her own experiences and convictions, was necessary in order to understand the world and how she could play a part in improving it. Understand the past, the present, and the future, and the connection between them. Understand how she should treat others and how she herself should be treated. And understand how she could improve herself and her own actions. All the things that contributed to the continued development of a being.

13

Orion carefully penned the final sentence before he looked at Chunlian with gratitude. He felt greatly inspired by this little being. Whether it was caused by the place of learning or by something that had always been present in her, she certainly had a gift for teaching.

Orion and Chunlian sat together in silence enjoying the comfortable atmosphere between them. After a while Chunlian looked seriously at Orion and said: "It is also important to understand that one can never reach the end of learning. I mean, during the cell time the goal was to learn the symbols of learning. And when that goal had been reached, many knowing ones thought that they had learned all there was to learn on the planet. That they had reached the pinnacle of achievement. They had never been told that there was more than that. They had never been presented with a perspective that showed that there was more in the world than the knowledge the wise ones taught. And since the knowing ones did not know any better, they thought that they knew everything.

"What I am trying to say is that one must never believe that one knows all there is to know. If one believes so, it only reveals a lack of insight into the greater perspective, in which what one does know is so very little. Because as soon as one gains more knowledge, one simultaneously discovers much more of which one is ignorant. And if a place of learning trains some who believe that they have learned everything there is to know, something is terribly wrong. One can never reach the end of learning, although during the cell time it was assumed that this was possible.

"Rather, in a place of learning one should train the learners in having an open mind, curiosity, and a belief that many other perspectives exist apart from one's own or that of a few.

"Once I had understood this and assumed an open mind, it was as if doors to the perspectives of others suddenly opened to me. Perspectives that I could take myself. Perspectives that helped me understand why those who saw through these perspectives thought and acted as they did.

"These perspectives, which were different, but equally as valid as my own, belong to my two friends, whom I want you to meet."

She stood up from the bench in front of the place of learning and walked slowly down along the white path. Orion smiled, knowing that he certainly possessed a curious mind. He almost could not wait to meet the two unfamiliar beings. Moreover, he felt immensely grateful for the kindness with which he had been met by everyone he had encountered. Was it perhaps the luminous planet that infused everyone with a radiant kindness? Or was it the beings themselves who possessed the kindness and in turn influenced the planet? Either way it was obvious that a foundation of goodness existed on the planet and in its inhabitants. And that this made Orion even more curious to discover how this foundation had been laid and how long it had existed.

14

Havar and Raven peered curiously through the round windows in their home. They had not seen a stranger for a very long time.

"I'll get the door," said Raven, who was very excited about this meeting.

Orion had just said goodbye to Chunlian when his eye caught a sudden movement from inside one of the large objects nearly. A movement of something opening up before him. Orion approached the place and his eyes suddenly opened wide. Two very different beings had appeared before him, emerging from within the large object. One was small, with dark hair and skin the colour of hazelnuts. It looked at Orion with a friendly, understanding expression in brown eyes that twinkled from a characteristic face. The other being was taller, but more slender and with hair as bright as the clearest star. It regarded Orion appraisingly, but he also sensed a critical glint in the gaze of the elegant, bright being. The three of them stood and looked at each other until Raven, who had opened the door, asked who Orion was.

"I am Orion," he replied.

"How interesting," Raven said and looked at Havar. She continued: "And what has brought you here?"

Orion hesitated. "It was not an action based on a random idea," he offered tentatively.

"I see. And tell me, Orion, have you fled from a planet, or are you here of your own free will?"

"Oh, Raven. Ask Orion to come into our home, and spare him the endless questions," Havar said to Raven, who knotted her brows.

Orion gaped in astonishment as he stepped into their home. In the centre of the circular room, a staircase wound its way from floor to ceiling. The staircase was a living tree whose branches harmoniously formed the steps. When using the stair, one moved with the tree closer to the sky.

Surrounding the growing centre were many plants of different kinds and sizes. Some carried fruit, others flowers, and others again only large, dark green leaves. The walls were made of wood and were lit in a beautiful reddish tone by the sun shining through the round windows. This home appeared to be alive. It contained so many little different elements that together formed a unified whole. It seemed that each little different part was necessary in order to achieve the complete whole. Orion had never before thought that this was possible, but rather thought that differences made unity impossible. Apparently, it was not so.

"Pensive he seems to be," Raven whispered to Havar, who was busy watering the many plants.

"What a lot of conclusions you draw today," he replied.

"He said that his journey here was not an action based on a random idea. Perhaps he is ... Do you think that he is ...?"

"Quiet, Raven," Havar hushed, before whispering: "The answer lives in the future, you know that. It is no use trying to rush it, on the contrary. We must give Orion the time he needs before he himself and any other knows it. All we can do is tell him the stories of our own pasts and *spare* him our questions. Do you hear me?"

Raven sighed and went to Orion. She offered him a seat. When Orion was seated, Raven told him that she and Havar did not originally come from the luminous planet.

"Just like the other beings," Orion added.

Raven looked pensive. "So you have spoken to others. That must mean that ..."

"Raven!" Havar exclaimed.

"I'm sorry. As I was saying, we do not come from here, but from two different planets that have in common that they are not in any way like this one. I am sure that you are interested in hearing our stories." Raven smiled when Orion immediately nodded vigorously. She looked at Havar and gestured for him to begin.

15

"Darkness is followed by light. A dark tunnel it is only with a white end. Night dies when day is born. After what felt like eternal ages of evil, darkness, and hatred, the day of light finally dawned. I arrived at the luminous planet, where we are currently assembled, during a time when my eyes had known too much darkness.

"I sensed a shock going through my body, and suddenly I was lying in a yellow field which in some mysterious way appeared as a reflection of the deep blue sky. A magical place, I thought. I winced, my mind was hurting. I looked around me and expected to see the things I was used to. But there was nobody there, neither the 5 walls that separated unhappy souls from each other so one half was abused while the other half would never be so. It was quiet here and no sound of the booming thunderous voice that constantly desired injustice between the planet's two races, as they were called. On the contrary, the place was full of a sense of peace as if it had never experienced the unending confusion, fear, and frustration I had heard in the high-pitched screams. I stood up and suddenly caught sight of something lying further ahead in the field. When I got closer I saw that it moved, and I asked if it needed help."

Havar paused and looked at Raven, who continued: "How is it possible to create a whole if part of it is excluded?"

Havar went on: "The strange being's words left me confused. Who was she, and where did she come from? Her phrase I recognised immediately, because I had also been carrying it with me for a long time. Its truth had frustrated me, because nobody who knew about it dared to speak it out loud. Apparently, I was wrong. Had this stranger experienced the same as me?"

Raven continued: "Before me stood a small being with dark eyes that radiated that they too had seen darkness. Nevertheless, he looked at me kindly and asked if I needed help. I could tell by his understanding gaze that he would listen to the eager voice of my heart, and so I spoke. I sensed his confusion, but not whether he agreed or disagreed with my statement."

"I agreed," Havar added.

"Yes, and you told me as much. That's why I shared my confusion with you. I did not know where I was, nor when I had arrived. I remembered fleeing from my planet when nothing but inequality ruled. It was horrific. I, along with the majority of my people, was apparently so different that we deserved nothing. We were made so different from the ideal that we lost our faith in ourselves and took upon us a deep doubt of life itself. The planet's beings were divided into 10 unequal groups. The first group contained the most 'right' beings; the tenth the most 'wrong'. Those of us who were most 'wrong' suffered under terrible conditions. We received no support or care, but only hatred and blame. Either we were born in the wrong place, where the conditions were terrible, or we had in the course of our life become so wrong that we ourselves were to blame for belonging to the lowest group.

"A few others, on the other hand, were born in the right places or became right during the course of their life, and they achieved wonderful conditions in their group. They had resources in excess: treasures, opportunities, food. These few owned everything, and the many owned nothing. The planet housed a colossal injustice that soon became impossible for the individual to oppose."

Raven hesitated, and Orion noticed a sadness reach her eyes. It was quiet among them for a while. Havar broke the silence with his calm voice: "In a similar way, injustice had grown on the planet I came from. The two races I told you about were likewise deemed right or wrong. But in my planet's case it was already decided before birth and there was nothing one could do about one's fate. It was fixed. I had a sister with whom I experienced, shared, and learned everything. We were born at the same time and grew up in the same place. In certain ways we were like one soul living in two bodies. At one in agreement and identity. But in other ways unique differences existed between us, the duality of which created a fascinating balance that none of us could have made on our own. Those around us had foretold that we as brother and sister would walk hand in hand along the same path of light. But they were wrong.

"It began with a dark feeling that evolved into an idea and transformed further into an evil deed. The dark and convincing thunderous voice spread its message throughout the whole planet and brain-washed those who desired to become the dominant race. *The difference between the two races must have consequences!* A notion was created that the dominant race had more innate worth, possessed better abilities, and should be revered because of this.

"My twin sister and I were sitting in our home when the injustice of the thunderous voice banged open the door. They accused me of being in the same room as my sister without further ado. That she did not deserve this special treatment but must imme-diately be exploited like all of her race. *She must know her place!* They dragged her out of the door, because neither she nor I in our state of terror had time to process what was going on. Her desperate eyes called to me for help, but I stood paralysed with shock. I never saw her again.

"Every day I, like everyone else belonging to the dominant race, heard the screams upon approaching the five walls that kept the two races separate. It would be impossible to penetrate the walls because each wall was taller than the next. But I knew that my sister was being kept over there, and I never left the walls. Something in me hoped that she would one day break out of there. I did not know for certain what took place on the other side of the five walls. But I was sure that they had it far worse than us. I could tell by their screams that they were being treated mercilessly by those of my race who controlled them. That their rights, their autonomy, and their opportunities had been taken away from them. These screams sounded constantly for a long time, until suddenly something terrifying happened. It went quiet. All at once, all sounds ceased on the other side of the walls, and I shuddered as I realised the truth that lay before me. They had given up.

"I left the five walls and miserably regarded the world, the half world that I now belonged to. There were no differences. The planet was controlled by one race, which had now won its final victory. It felt frightening and empty at the same time. Where was the duality? The balance, the equality between the two races?

"Why would anyone want to suppress and exclude a part of the population? Kill half of a whole? Couldn't they see that it would inevitably strike back at them and ultimately become a disadvantage?

"In the world I saw, I was the only one who realised this truth. It was impossible to awaken the reason in the minds that the thunderous voice had already brainwashed with selfishness and lies.

"It was soon thereafter that I arrived at the luminous planet. And after meeting Raven, whose past in many ways resembled my own, we made a shared decision that would impact the entire development on this planet."

Orion smiled and looked out through the window. They had contributed to the beauty that he saw in the planet's luminous centre. The decision they had made must have been the right one. He turned his attention to them again, as Havar said: "We had both realised what a catastrophe inequality causes. What a hindrance it is to the sustainable development of a place. What a deathly darkness it brings with it. Therefore, we decided that we wanted to fight ceaselessly for ensuring that the darkness of inequality would never overcome the light again. We wanted to fight for the creation of a place where equality would forever exist. Because we cannot create a whole if we exclude part of it."

Raved added: "And we achieved our goal. On this planet everyone is different but contributes equally to the unified whole. In our differences we are made one."

16

Orion thanked Raven and Havar for their generosity of words. He was very impressed with their point of view, which had opened new doors to understanding in his mind.

They welcomed him to stay with them, but Orion felt that he needed to spend some time alone with his thoughts. They said goodbye, and Orion left their circular home.

Outside, the evening had fallen, and the night sky proudly showed its face. It smiled at Orion, and he looked back at it in admiration. He began to walk along the white path that almost mirrored the light of the stars. He walked in silence, enjoying the peace resting in the night.

After a while he caught sight of a light that he had not seen before. It flickered in warm hues. It moved in time with the gentle breeze and endlessly changed shape. Orion approached it warily. The closer he got to the strange light, the warmer it felt. He now saw that it shone from inside the earth, as if a ray of the sun had landed just there. He admired this mysterious warmth and did not notice what surrounded it: all around the flames of the bonfire seventeen stones were laid in a near-perfect circle. When Orion's gaze fell upon them, he gaped in surprise as he took in the beautiful colours of the stones. The flames illuminated the stones with a golden glow and made the red, yellow, green, and blue shades appear truly magical.

Orion stepped into the circle of stones and felt a rush pass through his body.

"What's going on?" he asked out loud.

In that moment, the bonfire again demanded his attention by emitting a tall flame that took the shape of two half-circles. They approached each other, but just when the fire almost joined in a full circle, the two halves moved apart and remained halves. The flames repeated this pattern faster and faster. Orion, who had fallen to the ground as the fire startled him, stood up and moved closer to the wild flames. In an instant he suddenly understood that *only he* could bring the two halves together. He lifted both his hands and took a firm step toward the flames. His hands felt warmer, but he did not draw back.

Instead, he closed his eyes, and the image of the two half-circles approaching each other appeared in his mind. Orion took a deep breath and intensely desired to transform the divided into a whole. Suddenly he saw the two fiery halves unite into a great circle. Orion opened his eyes and saw before him a ring of fire that shone so brightly that it blinded him. He fell backwards and everything turned white.

17

"I sense that you are awake."

Orion slowly opened his heavy eyelids that hid the sight of the unfamiliar voice. He caught his breath when he saw the being standing before him. Its skin was white as snow, but where the eyes should have been there were instead two pitch-black scars. Orion shivered in aversion, but he could not take his eyes off the horrific sight.

The being moved closer to him, and Orion tried to get up, but he was still too dizzy. It felt as if the hollow, empty eyes looked straight at him and in some magical way enabled the being to move straight toward him.

Orion felt so scared that he let out a sharp yell as the being spoke again: "Do not be afraid at the sight of me."

It was now so near Orion that he could have reached out and touched the darkness that existed in place of the two eyes, had he dared.

"I mean you no harm, Orion, quite the contrary. You have lain here on the bench under the tree all night. I found you near The Final Place yesterday evening, and I was sure that you needed help. I did not know how long you had been lying there, so I brough you at once to my home. You were burning hot, so I thought you would need some fresh air. And that you got. I think you're already feeling better, am I right?"

Orion mumbled a few nonsensical words in his increasing confusion. At first he had thought he had awoken on his own star with its familiar eighteen walls cradling his little universe of books and comfort. And suddenly he remembered that he had met the six beings who had all told him their precious stories. But Orion could not remember what had brought him to this being. The Final Place? Suddenly an image appeared in his mind.

"A perfect circle!" Orion exclaimed.

The being tilted its head as if trying to understand, before saying: "Interesting. I sense that the moment for expanding on this statement is soon to come, and that it is related to The Final Place. But now is not that moment. Because right now I want to ask you to come with me. There is something I want to tell you."

Orion felt slightly less anxious about the being who had helped him and shown him this great kindness. He slowly got up from the bench and decided to follow the being, who was already moving ahead on the white path. Suddenly it stopped, and Orion saw why. They were at the end of a very tall staircase, whose top must reach far into the sky.

Inexplicably, the staircase stood there in the middle of nowhere, and Orion was so absorbed in looking at it that he barely realised that the being was on its way up. Without thinking, Orion hurried after the being up the many stairs.

"Wait," Orion called, short of breath.

As his confusion about the staircase grew, Orion became more and more dizzy. It seemed like the stair would never end. Every time Orion thought he was nearing the top, another flight of steps began, forcing Orion to continue upwards.

It was a long time since he had lost sight of the other being, and several times he had nearly given up. He had reached a point where he could no longer feel his feet, but only see that they still moved. At the same time, he sensed something else: mysterious thoughts in his mind.

Is it possible to fight if one cannot see the goal? If a staircase loses a step, is it possible to reach the top?

Orion pressed his eyes together and tried to understand these thoughts, while he was still running up the stairs. Amid the black he saw an image before him: rotating stairs. He was looking down at them from above. They spun faster and faster, until it seemed that all the steps melded into each other and became a moving circle. Then Orion was no longer viewing the stair from above but was caught in its centre. He wanted the spinning steps to stop so he could climb on and escape. One by one to reach the top. If he did not manage this, he would be trapped in the centre of the stair forever. He felt sure of this. The spinning circle created a strong wind around

Orion, and he struggled to keep his balance. Orion had lost his perspective and could no longer see his goal. He looked dejectedly at the rotating circle and noticed a gap in it as if one of the steps was missing.

Another mysterious idea entered Orion's mind: If the jump is too high, are there some goals that can never be reached? Or is there always a solution? Is it possible to create one's own step or repair or rethink?

Orion suddenly realised that he himself was the only solution that could bring him out of the spinning circle. He had to fill the gap in the circle. In his mind, Orion ran towards the incomplete circle and was filled with an enormous sense of unity. He discovered that he was now part of the circle. He filled the gap that had been between the steps. For a moment Orion flowed with the circle of steps and moved upwards. The circle spun slower now, until all the steps finally came to a halt. Orion continued up towards the top of the stairs, without looking back, because he did not need to see for himself; he knew that the staircase was a complete whole.

A strong wind hit Orion and woke him from his thoughts. He looked up and discovered that there were no more steps. He had reached the top of the stairs. Beside him stood the being, although Orion barely recognised it. The black holes that had replaced its eyes were gone. Instead two large, shining dark blue eyes were looking directly at Orion. The being spoke with a resonant voice: "My name is

Parshi. I have brought you to the stair of perspective to show you what my eyes see."

He opened his arms, gesturing, and Orion gawped at the magnificent view. From here Orion could see the planet's centre but in a different perspective than before. He saw at the same time both details and wholes, heard laughter and silence. It was just like when he was back home on his star and as a spectator had admired the luminous planet. Except for one thing: Now he was both spectator and participant. He felt like a sphere whose centre is everywhere and circumference nowhere. It was as if everything was one. As if the distance between the stair of perspective and the centre of the luminous planet was non-existent. Orion had a feeling that the distance between everything in the entire universe was non-existent. Physically there was a distance, but on an inner level, independent of space and time, everything was one unity and therefore infinitely close.

"The thoughts that occupy your mind at this moment once also did so in mine. In fact, in all 17 of us beings who before you have scaled the many flights of stairs," Parshi said. He went on: "The perspective that the staircase gives us creates a new mindset in us. A mindset that brings us closer to an understanding of the whole. Listen, Orion, I have not always lived sightless. I come from a planet where I myself was responsible for losing it. I lived with my sight turned inward and paid no mind to anything but my own development, my own plans, and my own life. I lost the ability to see others and the necessity of working in cooperation with them. I became selfish and lived by the notion that I was independent of others. Eventually, I did not even *see* others. I cannot tell you if that was because they no longer existed, or if I simply did not focus on them, because I cannot remember. All I remember is that I was so engrossed in my own life that my sight ultimately became unnecessary. It disappeared.

"I had lived unconsciously in a dark fog in which only my own thoughts illuminated the grey. Without sight I saw this same fog, but the difference was that I no longer had the possibility to see anything else. My own inner self, that I had been so preoccupied with, became my prison. The difference between my own choice and having no choice terrified me.

"I desperately wanted to correct my selfish thoughts and actions, but it was too late. There was no hope for me. No hope, until the day that a bright green light that I had never seen before shone into my inner dark fog. I pursued it while hoping that it would give me another chance. I travelled far and never let the bright green light leave my mind.

"One day I bumped into something hard and discovered that it was a staircase. I climbed its countless steps all the way to the top. There, an incredibly beautiful sight overwhelmed me. I had eyes again, and this time it was eyes that looked beyond my own horizon. At that moment one thing was entirely clear to me: If one desires to achieve an ideal, it is only possible through cooperation.

"I decided to live my life by this realisation, and now I strive to create and maintain cooperation between everyone here on our luminous planet. I show this place at the top of all the many stairs to those who need to realise the necessity of cooperation, that cooperation is crucial if we want to reach a common goal. This place possesses an ability to show those who have ascended the perspective and the insight that already reside within them." Parshi's deep blue eyes shone before they turned to Orion with a serious gaze.

"However, the greed and selfishness of my past have had consequences. The terrifying sight of the black scars takes the place of the sight of my eyes. Sometimes it looks even darker when I also lose my inner sight. My perspective."

A small sigh from Orion expressed his compassion for Parshi's plight. But Parshi simply smiled and continued: "Whenever I lose perspective, I can always climb these many stairs that so generously give me back my sight and show me a pure perspective. Never forget, Orion: Even one who has made the biggest mistake, life will regard with its merciful eyes."

Beholding this scene from afar, from the universe's seat, one would see two happy beings, observing and being part of a lively, busy landscape. They smiled contentedly, pleased at all the cooperation they saw and the feeling of unity that they felt. From this distant seat, far, far away in the universe, one would sense that everything had in this instant become a little more beautiful. Everything seemed a little brighter.

18

An infinite universe. Thus it is described. If the universe is truly infinite, we may imagine that everything in the universe is repeated or is happening in several places at once, since the infinite universe would contain endless possibilities. That *everything* is taking place simultaneously means that all conceivable possibilities of action exist at the same time. For this to be possible, several different universes must exist in the same place. *Parallel universes*. But if several universes exist at the same time in the same place, reality must have more than three dimensions. In this way, the perhaps countless dimensions of the universe overlap, take place at the same time, and perhaps influence each other.

In an infinite universe with this possible truth, one universe might by its influence inspire or change the future of another universe.

Orion shivered and shook off the odd sensation. A mysterious, almost frightening sense had suddenly come over him while he was looking up into the glowing night sky. A strange idea that Orion could barely grasp.

It was impossible to describe exactly, but he had somehow felt that he was not the only one. That this night sky or this planet was not the only one. As if something similar, but also opposite, also existed.

But not that it would exist in the future, or had existed in the past. No, it existed exactly now, parallel to Orion's thoughts right at this moment.

He shook his head again, trying to send the indefinable notion on its way.

As he did so, Orion suddenly felt a humid breeze, and as he turned around he caught sight of an unfamiliar being. As always, an overwhelming sense of curiosity bubbled up inside Orion, displacing the strange feeling from before.

19

The unfamiliar being was clad all in blue. Its dark, wavy hair flew wildly in the wind. The blue eyes were hard to read. Their expression seemed to be both content and longing at the same time.

After a while in silent observation, something dramatic happened. Like a flash flood, the being suddenly burst into tears. The life in the tears revealed a dreadful past, the injustice of which had been ignored for too long.

Despite the upheaval of its emotions, the being began to speak, its voice clearly moved. Its name was Tahi. Tahi had lived on the luminous planet for a long time, but admitted that something kept him from feeling the same about the planet's light as the other beings did. He told how he was ashamed over this feeling, because seen with the eyes of reason there was no grounds for feeling so. Here it was clear to him that he lived in a world that ought to be ideal. He was surrounded by beauty and loving beings. He ought to feel good. But this prickling sense that something was missing, or rather, that something had to disappear, kept him from feeling as he ought. Tahi believed that his sorrow originated in a sense of being connected to something undesired, but unfortunately also unknown. And it was this undesired sense of longing in a soul who couldn't find the reason for feeling it, that like a chain held Tahi back from reaching the fullness of the planet's joy.

20

The first rays of the sun beamed down. The dew of night slowly awoke and began to depart from the cosy blankets of the green leaves. A scent of energy and a sense of calm blended and created the beauty that resides in every morning.

Orion and Tahi had been sitting beneath a mighty tree through the night. Endless had been their wonder, discussions, and eventually understandding. Absorbed in each other's ideas they had forgotten all about time and place and had lived this night in their own universe. Tahi had told Orion why he had journeyed to the luminous planet. Told how he had lived on a planet whose merciless fate had become unbearable. Sometime during this tale, Orion had remembered the mysterious feeling he had felt the moment before he had encountered the then unknown Tahi.

"An identical, but simultaneously opposite universe existing parallel to ours?" Tahi had asked.

Under the stars of the night they had discussed the strange idea, and the further they moved into the clarity of understanding, the more alive they felt.

"What if there are more variations of me that I am connected to without being aware of it?" Tahi said.

They both sat for a while and pondered this. A thought flooded into Orion's mind and carefully he began to examine it. What if Tahi had never entirely left behind the planet of his past? If part of him still lived there? Could it be possible that he had travelled to the luminous planet after his previous planet had been killed, but that another reality existed in a different universe, in which he still lived on his previous planet? What if he was in some way connected to this alternative reality whose mood, feelings, or thoughts continued to affect him? If he was bound to another life that in a way was his own, but in this current reality was impossible for him to control. Orion smiled. Or was it?

21

One last tear fell into the dying ocean. The few waves that could still be seen glittered as a colourless rainbow. Dirty hues of grey and black formed the dominant mass that spread everywhere as a deadly disease. Soon the entire sea would be covered by the glinting, poisonous matter. The tear became one with the waves and briefly lent them a shimmer of naturalness before it too was absorbed into the merciless poison that kills all hope.

Tahi, who was sitting aboard a small boat of rotting wood, leaned forward, hopelessly searching for something that could save him, not knowing what. It seemed impossible, almost foolish, to keep believing that the ocean could be saved. Waste and pollution clogged the surface of the water as far as the eye could see. Out of sight below the surface, the garbage probably extended deep, deep down towards the bottom and would before long take over the role as the planet's ocean. It would keep spreading until the last drop of seawater had dried up and been replaced with waste so dense that nothing would be able to remove it. Then the ocean would be for ever destroyed and the toxic mass of waste would fill the wide expanses that had previously contained a healthy and pure ocean.

Tahi's skin had gradually changed to a brighter colour than white and the circles around his eyes to a darker colour than black. He no longer looked like a living being. No longer felt like one. He signed and paddled back towards the shore with slow movements.

Seen from above, Tahi looked like just another spot of waste in the poisoned ocean. And he felt just as meaningless. It was this shocking truth that was encountered by a being that was both identical and opposite to the living, bright spot on the sea.

Slowly this being moved closer to himself. He was in a small boat without room for two. He settled on the railing, and the boat tipped.

The unbalancing interrupted Tahi who quickly turned around. His eyes met the strange and at once familiar being. Silence fell. Even the few waves on the sea and the creaking noises of the waste around the boat ceased.

They sat close together in each end of the boat. It was as if through the confused and curious eyes of the other they entered each other's unfamiliar universes. Tahi peered into the depth and saw in the eyes of the other being a light so radiant that he was filled with a profound sense of hope. He examined this light and perceived that it had its origin in something vast. It looked like a star but shone much warmer. Suddenly he realised that it was a planet. Through the eyes of the other being, Tahi moved closer to this luminous planet, gaping at the sight that met him. The circumference of the planet was alight with hues of gold so bright that Tahi had to squint to be able to look at it directly. On the planet itself, the soil, trees, rivers, and oceans emitted a wonderful sense of balance. The entire vision appeared deeply inviting. But what astonished Tahi the most was the beings who lived on the luminous planet: happy and free beings that radiated an enormous love for life. Tahi realised that life on this planet was the only reality that it was right to live in.

In the middle of this joyful realisation, Tahi noticed some elongated objects that cast a sinister shadow over one of the beings on the planet. On closer inspection, Tahi identified them as 14 chains. The end of each chain was connected to this being, who now bore an expression of longing sadness. But Tahi could not see what the other end of the chains were fastened to. He looked at the chained being again and let out a gasp when he noticed that the being was looking right back at him.

Shocked, Tahi pulled away from the vision. He tumbled backwards in the boat and nearly fell into the poisoned water. But he didn't fall, because something held him back. He looked about, confused. And he saw that fourteen chains were fastened to his own foot. The ends of the being's chains were linked to himself.

Tahi sat up and met the friendly gaze of the being once more. He understood. Slowly but surely, he loosened the heavy chains from his foot and gratefully breathed in the freedom.

Time stood still, but the thoughts passing between the two in the boat moved infinitely quickly. At the same moment, they smiled and left the other's universe forever.

The being that had arrived in Tahi's boat took a deep breath. Independence. Resolutely it pushed Tahi down into the deadly depth. The being smiled kindly. There was only room for one. Around him, Tahi felt the rotting wood of the boat heal up and get stronger, as if growing anew. Freedom. And in that moment, the being Tahi set out towards the brightest future.

Sahar sat smiling on one of the wooden chairs. She was part of a group of other laughing beings but radiated a particular uniqueness that made her stand out from the others. It was as if she glowed with pride and humility at the same time. It was clear that she enjoyed her surroundings and moved as if she was doing all she could to take care of them. She sat on the simple wooden chair as if it were the most precious work of art. And while the others talked, she now and then looked around her and smiled to herself. She made anyone curious to learn what had caused her obvious love for this place.

And then she told her tale. With a deep sense of joy, she began to speak about her arrival on the luminous planet. She had been studying the planet from a distance at times when, for the sake of her heart's survival, it had been necessary to look away from her own planet. In her imagination, she escaped to the luminous planet that shone with hope and fresh ideas. Two things that did not exist on the planet on which she was trapped. With her head tilted back she admired the luminous planet and came to bear a great love for it. She imagined the life and energy that resided on it, and was filled with a deep sorrow every time she was reminded of the place where she was still bound.

She would say goodbye to her dreams and turn her face back to the harsh reality in which she lived. As a centre of the many tall and dark constructions, she passed through the landscape that she had known for so long. Earthy brown clouds of smog surrounded her on the outside and slowly poisoned her on the inside. A rotting city was what she lived in. Filth and waste were building up and drew foul insects and deadly diseases to the city. It was impossible to think a single positive thought in this place that with every moment devoured the hopes and dreams of its people.

A people that had long ago realised that they were themselves to blame for the fate of the city. Yet, action, improvement, and rescue seemed to them either impossible or not worth the effort. In any case, the people had done nothing to change the fate of their city in a more positive direction. All they had done was to accept it. An action that would never deliver them from their misery.

Sahar, on the other hand, had as a solitary minority fought with all her might. She refused to accept the slow death that the city was headed towards. She did everything in her power to persuade people of the necessity for positive action but was met with nothing but cold walls. All roads were blind alleys and led only to a stubborn impasse. Not a single crack or opening was there to allow her hope to pass through and carry on. In the end, she nearly lost hope herself, which is why she in her mind sought to escape from the city's catastrophic deterioration and the threatening, dark clouds that surrounded her body.

One day Sahar had been sitting on a sharp kerbstone near a stinking pile of refuse. She had looked up towards the clouded sky in an attempt to catch a glimpse of the luminous planet. Suddenly, 11 large and pitch-black buzzing swarms of aggressive insects had floated across the sky, in an instant blotting out the last light of the day.

Sahar knew at once what this meant: The end of the planet. The black swarms were deadly and poisoned anyone within seconds of engulfing them. Their buzzing hurt the ears and almost drowned out the sound of the many screams and howls of pain that Sahar heard all around her. She was helpless but calm. As a rock in a storm she regarded the chaos surround-dding her. The people who had refused to act on the mounting problems in the city had now finally been roused and were running about fuelled by an incredible energy. It was as if they only now, so close to the ultimate end, had realised the city's value and the necessity of its survival. Now they were prepared to fight. They wanted to save the city from the dark and poisonous clouds that had been left to grow and spread for so long. Now they wanted to save the planet. But this now was too late. The battle was over before it had even begun for the planet's people. One by one they fell to the filthy ground, their eyes filled with a hope that might once have saved them but had appeared far too late. The city had been killed by its own people.

As the last person standing, Sahar felt the silence that came after the poisonous buzzing. Emptiness grew. Sahar looked up at the sky and noticed a tiny opening in the dark cover of smog. Through the opening she suddenly perceived a glimmer whose light was calling to her. She fell down.

When she came to, she was lying on a patch of bright white stones and looked up into a clear blue sky. She breathed in the fresh air and heard the whispers of trees in the gentle breeze. She smiled, knowing at once where she was.

The luminous planet was far more beautiful than she had ever imagined in her dreams. She looked around her and quickly developed a deep love for the wonderful place where she was. She walked along a path, so white and fine, which with every step she took made her ever fonder of all that she beheld. Suddenly she was stirred by a feeling that she had to do whatever she could to prevent a similar catastrophe to the one that had gripped her former planet from taking place here. She knew how unfair it was that an innocent planet fell victim to the actions of thoughtless creatures. She promised herself, and all the beauty that she saw around her, that she would build a city that would never meet such a terrible fate. A city that would forever blossom. A sustainable city. And she realised this dream.

Sahar was connected to the society she had created. She considered places of habitation, places to be, to develop, and to learn, that all inhabitants of the luminous planet could enjoy and use. Consideration of the planet was always at the centre of what she created. Everything had to benefit it and must never become a burden. Through respect for the planet and the thoughtfulness that guided the construction of its city, Sahar achieved her goal: The creation of a sustainable city.

Words. Words dancing over the undulating crests of letters and hum their way across the peaceful pastures of spaces. Words that smile as they take form. Words that belong. Words that link and create connection, light up and enlighten. In other words: Words that make sense.

Orion's words were beginning to take shape. His writings and notes about the beings, impressions, and experiences on the luminous planet had learned to walk and were soon running swiftly across the blank pages he had brought with him from his star. He looked down at the pages on which the newly completed sentences about Sahar rested. Below the many words the rest of the paper was quite empty. He tried to imagine what letters would settle there, what tales they would carry.

He shrugged. It was impossible to predict. Nothing on this journey had been predictable. And yet, Orion admitted to himself that he had predicted a long tale before he had even departed for the luminous planet. A tale whose simplicity was now laid bare and revealed that it had far from been able to contain of all the activity that had taken place so far. He looked at the remaining blank pages and smiled to himself. He was looking forward to seeing the unpredictable words smiling back at him.

When Orion looked up from his papers towards Sahar, who had been sitting across from him as she told her story, the chair was suddenly empty. He looked around, but she was not in sight. Instead, several other beings had arrived at The Round Place, as Sahar had called it. Orion saw Raven and Tahi who waved at him before they also sat down. Orion recognised more faces and noticed Chunlian, Terra, and Agua in the middle of a discussion that appeared to claim their full attention. Orion sensed that something momentous was about to happen in this place. Yet, the three beings were so caught up in their conversation that they did not appear to notice what was going on around them.

"So you claim that evolution is eternal?" Terra asked pensively.

"Yes," Agua replied, before Chunlian added: "And you believe that evolution is the reason we are here?"

Agua gazed up at the sky for a moment before she calmly replied: "That is true. I believe so. But I know that it is something that I believe."

"What do you mean?" asked Chunlian.

"It is not something that I believe that I know."

They smiled at each other, and Agua spoke again: "I cannot know it with absolute certainty, but I choose to believe in my experiences, which all tell me that everything I see is in the process of evolving. I cannot think of anything in this world that is standing still. I cannot see anything that is not evolving towards something better in the end."

"If everything that you see in the world is evolving, does the same apply to everything in the universe as a whole?"

Agua thought for a moment. "Neither can I claim to know this. Because everything is so much greater than I, and I cannot say anything that even approaches the truth thereof. Therefore I'll not say anything. But what I can say something about is what I experience and observe in the world, and everything that meets my eyes strives towards evolution. From the flower that sprouts in order one day to blossom, to us who learn in order one day to understand."

"But why does this evolution exist?" Chunlian asked, now more keen.

"Perhaps it is simply because it makes us better than we were before we evolved, and this is preferable?"

They fell silent.

After a while, Terra said: "When I think about it, I also notice a pattern in all the things I observe. For example, look at our previous planets; it was obvious to all of us that evolution was necessary, for both survival and well-being. Realisations and ensuing actions had to set the evolution going, but disasters got the upper hand and the evolution was delayed.

But the conflicts did not eradicate it, because the evolution is continued here on the luminous planet. Indeed, it flourished when each one of us brought it here with us. The pattern that prevails everywhere in small as well as great things, is thus a pattern that ensures evolution no matter what happens. Everything that happens will either delay or hasten evolution, but, regardless, it will eventually proceed, perhaps even eternally. Thus, the way I see it, it does not make any sense to act against the force of evolution, since it will eventually win through no matter what. Indeed, it would be wiser to simply accept it and then to do everything possible to participate in its glorious pattern."

They sat in silence for another moment, before Chunlian once again looked at Agua and asked: "Is this the same pattern that you talk about when you say that evolution is eternal?"

"Yes, it is the same. But as I said before, I do not want to persuade you that it is true. My eyes do not reach far enough into the universe to see where the pattern we are talking about is manifest. But in the places that my eyes have seen, and my heart has sensed, I experience the pattern of eternal evolution with a radiant clarity. These experiences give me grounds for believing that evolution is eternal, and that we are here in the world in order to proceed with it towards something even greater. But which greater, and where it will lead, I do not know. But if I go along with the pattern of evolution, I believe that it will be even more wonderful than this place."

They smiled, and each sat with their own thoughts for a while. Then Chunlian asked one more question, peering into the distance: "Whether or not the universe is about evolution, I would still like to know why it exists instead of not existing. Is it simply because mass is preferable to void? Certainly there is a meaning that I am too small to grasp, so I am not wondering in order to know the meaning, but to know why there is a meaning at all, instead of no meaning. Why does everything exist instead of nothing? Is it just for fun? Or is my being also too small to comprehend the answer to this?"

Orion did not hear the answer to this question, because right at that moment Sahar came back with a chair for Orion. She told him that he was very welcome to sit here while it was happening, but that he was not eligible to participate in the decision-making, because he was not an expert in the areas – yet, of course, she added with a smile. Orion took a seat on the chair, slightly confused, but had no chance to ask questions. Just then, three beings arrived that Orion had never seen before, and all fell silent at once.

25

Between the six round wooden tables, each now surrounded by three chairs, a small platform marked the centre of The Round Place. Parshi, who had also just arrived, gently stepped onto the platform. Although his eyes were again replaced by the dark scars, it seemed that he sensed Orion's presence, because he gave a smile in his direction. He breathed in and began to speak.

"Great decisions need to be made. It is important that we examine our thoughts carefully and scrutinise our solutions to the best of our ability. The stories of the three fates whose endings have yet to play out, are in many ways interwoven. Thus, the solutions to their problems cannot be regarded in isolation, because however they turn out in the end, they will as always affect many other stories than their own. They will have a particularly great impact on your stories, which is why you must be part of the solutions we have to find now."

All the beings looked around at each other and exchanged regards full of warmth, and they all looked ready to get started. But Parshi continued speaking, and Orion sensed that he probably mostly did it for his sake.

"As always, it is those who know the story best who must enlighten the rest of us on the most important points. In turn, we must listen and ask questions in order to understand the problem's gravity as well as possible. How we can prevent the problems in the stories from ever occurring here on the luminous planet, and how the solutions that we come up with will not create other problems elsewhere, is what we need to reflect on and discuss. And, besides, we must be constantly mindful that the problems do not make us myopic in our solutions. In other words, we should not only walk in the paths that the problems themselves present to us. Rather, we must allow ourselves to leave behind these confining tracks and step out into the open landscape where we have a greater vision, and where the richer view may be even more beautiful.

"We must not let our solutions be limited by what we do not believe is possible or what we have been afraid to try before. We must leave behind the mindset that originally created the problem, and dare to invent new solutions for the sake of the best possible future. Now, the time has come for us to discuss what solutions will be most beneficial to us all and to the planet, and then decide to act on the very best of them."

Following Parshi's words, The Round Place began to buzz with thoughtful discussion in the search for the most favourable solutions. Orion sat and observed the process on his chair, astonished and impressed with the cooperation that took place between the beings and their different points of view.

A being unfamiliar to Orion had stepped onto the round platform. The being's hair was black, and it had yellowish skin. Its movements were rapid, and it was impossible not to be struck by the enormous sense of energy it radiated. It looked around at the other beings assembled, a light in its great eyes that made Orion feel instantly invigorated in its presence. The being spoke with lightning speed, and Parshi several times had to indicate with a gesture that the being speak more slowly. At this, the being's face broke into a wide grin, but Orion could see that the being had to concentrate to control the powerful energy with which it spoke. The being's name was Nuki.

"The planet of my past only worked optimally with the aid of energy. Because we had arranged it so that almost all activity required energy. And we needed these areas of activity for our survival and development. Once we had lived without supplied energy, but that way of life was far more primitive, and most of us would have found it impossible to live like that again. Therefore, the energy that ensured the new and better way of life meant everything to us."

Nuki paused for a moment before continuing his tale. "There were two ways of obtaining energy. One of them was like drinking from a glass, where the amount of water is limited. The other way was like slaking one's thirst at a waterfall, where the water is in a perpetual flow. Of course, the latter method is preferable, but nevertheless the first method was used to an unwholesome degree."

"But why? It is obvious that it makes no sense to overuse something from a limited source," Sahar asked critically.

Nuki sighed. "First of all because the first method had been known longest. And for a long time there had been a merciless game going on of finding this limited source. Because its contents were incredibly precious and those who found it would become abundantly wealthy. And since power follows wealth, it is not hard to figure out why the use of the energy from the limited source kept on being a factor, although it would turn out to be a toxic process. A process that polluted the planet to a terrifying and unimaginable degree.

"Yet, many realised the problem of using the limited source and drawing on its polluting energy, and many alternative methods were developed for obtaining and using energy from sources that were sustainable and healthy. This was of enormous importance. It became glaringly obvious that it was these sustainable methods that would supply the energy of the future for all activities on the planet. But if this transition was to be accomplished, the new methods would have to be further developed, and for this to happen they would require the complete support from all involved.

"But that never happened. Because incomprehensible and inexplicable is the act of one who is made blind by wealth. Those who had been players in the game of chasing the limited source, did not wish to give up all chances of future gain. But the more wealth they accumulated by using the energy from the limited source, the more dire were the consequences of doing so. They were sacrificing themselves, because in their innermost heart they knew that the disastrous consequences would strike even them one day. But even worse was that they sacrificed every other being, including the planet, in their pursuit of wealth."

Sahar said that she understood the reasoning, and Nuki continued: "But whether the energy came from a limited or a renewable source, there was also a huge imbalance in the way the energy was distributed. It was far from everybody who had access to energy, and the beings who lacked were therefore doomed to live in the out-dated, primitive way of life."

"Who were the victims of this unfair distribution?" Raven asked.

"The planet was separated into many different areas, and some areas were far more vulnerable than others. Vulnerable in all kinds of ways. And to add to the injustice, it was the beings living in these vulnerable areas that also lacked access to energy," Nuki replied.

Chunlian cleared her throat before asking: "You said that almost all activity on the planet required energy. But if it had been possible to live without energy before, was it not possible, for the sake of the planet, to go back and live in the same way again, although it was primitive?"

"Energy was mainly used in 7 ways: where we lived, where we learned, where we healed, where we created food, where we worked, where we undertook transportation, and where we communicated. Before we discovered that we could use energy to improve these areas, they had existed, but only in a far inferior degree. It was incredible the way that energy could improve every one of these areas and make them, for example, even more successful or more safe. So to answer your question, stopping the energy used in these areas would reduce the well-being of the planet's beings to such a great extent that it could not possibly be the right thing to do. A balance had to be struck. Without energy it would be like taking a step back in evolution. It was right that we made use of energy. Just not in the way that we were doing it."

The assembly fell silent for a moment. Orion thought he could guess how Nuki's story would end. And just as he had this thought, the energetic being's words continued flowing, and Orion listened once again.

"Yellow flashes of light and thunder was my last sight of the planet. It ended in a chaotic combustion in which only the black ash held the memory of the battle the good lost. A battle where reason had nothing to say, and where untruths and greedy ambition had dominated. A battle against the beings that ignored or even acted against a healthy use of energy and a just distribution of it to the benefit of all.

"At one point, all the dark energy of the battle had gathered in a dense, quaking mass. I managed to leave the planet in time. In time, before the dark energy spread across the whole planet and emitted an ominous light that made all wish that they had acted rationally long, long ago. But at this moment it was too late. The dark energy splintered in thousands of sparks. Electric, deadly colours painted the planet's destruction, and it was soon impossible to tell which regrettable acts had taken place there. Only I could carry on the story."

And that he had now done. When Nuki had spoken the last words, his face emphatically radiated the necessity of finding a healthy way of obtaining, consuming, and distributing the energy of the luminous planet. He smiled, because he knew that it was possible. Then his eyes caught those of a being that stood up in the same moment. As the being stepped onto the platform, Orion noticed its hands. They were red from scarring, and in many places the skin had been torn up. These hands were so worn that they must have been used far, far too much and far, far too long after it would have been wise to use them.

"My name is Matu," the being said and looked down at Orion. "The problem that engulfed my previous planet in many ways resembles Nuki's. In many places, I see my past in his words. I'll try to describe the gravity of the problem in a way that helps you understand why it is so important that things do not turn out the same way here. Why we must not make the same decisions and act in the same way that we did on the planet where I used to live."

Orion sensed that Matu was visualising the planet in his mind before speaking again.

"In the centre of the planet stood a great hall. Seen from the outside, it was a confusing sight: extensions and expansions of the hall had made it ever larger and the different architectural styles revealed that this had been going on for a long, long time. Originally, large, rough stones had formed the perimeter of the hall. Later, huge wooden poles had been used to expand the hall. Around these, the wood had been given new shape with detailed figures that embellished the surface of the wood. In other places one could see metal shaping the enormous facades. Colours and patterns of all kinds were also part of the hall's variegated appearance. But the hall, whose appearance signalled such an impression of countless

110

and diverse things, did not come close to matching the variety inside.

"Because inside the hall was a market that contained all things a being might need in life. And by 'things' I mean for example useful goods like warm clothing and furniture, but also food and water. At the beginning, the market had been simple and its goods limited. Only the most essential for the beings' survival was to be found there. But in the course of time the market had developed, and its goods had multiplied in kind, ingenuity, and utility. The goods ensured better lives for the planet's beings, and the development of the market continued. Eventually, the goods on the market had become so numerous that many of them were useless and redundant. But only rarely, or never, was any inspection of the goods undertaken, and there were in fact no rules or limits for the kinds of goods on the market. The market inside the hall thus became an immense, confusing world of things, useful and useless, created by and for the planet's beings."

Matu sighed before continuing. "I want to move straight to the problems that the market created: Firstly, excess consumption. The market's goods were made from the planet's resources. And the desire for more goods on the market caused a greater need for using the planet's resources. Eventually so great a need that it became unsustainable. If the beings were to continue living in the same way, their need for resources would require at least three planets to supply them.

"The second problem was the waste of goods. For example, when a being found that some goods were no longer desirable, or if they had been used and no longer functioned optimally, they were simply thrown away. There was no system in place to ensure that the goods would be reused, passed on to someone else, or turned into other kinds of goods. So a vast mountain outside the market grew and grew, a mountain of discarded goods. Wasted goods.

"The third problem was this: The unfair distribution of goods. Every night, the market was restocked with goods that had just been created, and there was plenty for every being to have what they needed. In the morning, the distribution of goods would commence. A distribution that ought to and easily could have been peaceful and fair.

"But every morning, when the planet's beings stood ready and waiting outside the doors, the atmosphere among them was always anxious. Negative words and greedy noises were uttered, and many beings shoved those standing near. Some were violent and fought their way closer to the hall's entrance with desperation painted in their face. Others needed neither to shove nor to worry, because they had secured a permanent spot at the front of the queue for the market's goods. Some used lies and tricks to cheat their way ahead in line. Others again simply gave up, and a few hoped for the best.

"And once the market's doors swung open, the anxious atmosphere was transformed into a barbaric chaos of selfish beings that feared not getting enough or desired to have more. It was a struggle for the market's goods, in which everyone took what they could get their hands on. Every morning held out the opportunity for a fair distribution in its open palms. But again and again, the beings chose to continue the story of how some got far too much, and others got far too little."

Matu looked out at the beings surrounding him. His eyes moved to Tahi, who asked: "What happened to the beings who never got enough of the goods they needed?"

"They lived a fate of constant lack. They went hungry and thirsty, they were poor and became desperate or hopeless. And what is worse, their number constantly increased. The number of beings on my previous planet was always escalating. Every day 12 new inhabitants arrived on the planet. This only aggravated the unjust distribution. More and more beings now had to share the goods of the market, but the just balance in which everyone got what they required, was never reached," Matu replied in a quiet voice.

Parshi nodded in understanding. Then he said: "Very well. Thank you, Matu. Now let us hear the last of you three, whose words are brothers and sisters."

Matu smiled and stepped off the platform. For a moment it was empty. Orion looked around at the beings surrounding him and noticed that they were all looking in the same direction. And then Orion also saw her. The first thing that caught his eye was her red hair that danced like flames around her lovely face. Even at a distance, he noticed the light in her green eyes. They shone with an expression of seeing the world through a great hope, and Orion immediately felt lighter. She wore a shimmering green dress that flowed around her bright legs as she walked towards the platform. Orion was overwhelmed by her expression that seemed so strong-willed, so certain. As if nothing in the world could challenge the act of hope that she used to paint her destiny. Orion would almost say that she stood like a mighty tree with a crown in full bloom. Then she spoke.

"Let these words be the last used to depict the toxic consequences of selfish and ignorant acts. Let them form the ending of our memories of planets that react to the thoughtless acts of their beings. Let them be the final picture in our minds of burning forests, poisoned drinking-water, dying oceans, polluted cities, alarming temperature changes following the misuse of energy, and overconsumption of limited resources.

"Let these words be the last spoken about the catastrophes that beings set in motion, perhaps believing that the serious consequences would never affect them. Consequences that they could in no way mitigate once it was too late. But it was already too late. Their planets ultimately had to show the beings that their endless ability to disregard the imminent catastrophe would eventually strike back at them. Because in the end, beings are not as great as their closed eyes make them believe. As soon as they open their eyes and see clearly, they discover that there is a whole world around them, a planet greater and older than themselves. They realise that it makes no sense to treat this planet as an isolated entity whose destruction means nothing. Whose fate is not part of their own. Because with their eyes open, they see that they are part of this planetary being. This is what we, too, must realise if we want to live on the luminous planet in such a way that natural disasters will never be sown, grow, or spread here."

She looked around at the others assembled, who all listened attentively to every word. Above them the clouds gathered slightly, as if creating a little room in which words about her past would soon find their place.

"Lima, what happened on your previous planet?" Parshi asked.

"Lima," Orion repeated silently to himself. Her name reminded him of a word, but in the moment he could not recall which. He looked into Lima's green eyes again, and she began her story.

"The planet of my past was a living being, both vulnerable and strong, just like the rest of us. Her beauty was indescribable and her voice priceless. We who lived with her had many reasons to be thankful. Her forests kept us alive and gave us shelter and heat. Her babbling brooks generously quenched our thirst. Her ocean was a treasure trove of magic, and when we saw our reflection in it we saw for a moment the same magic within ourselves. Our cities wandered over her tall mountains and sheltered valleys, gave us room to be. Her precious energy we could use for our benefit, and unconditionally she created more. Her soil she let blossom, her plants she let grow, and she allowed us to eat our fill of them. She kept us alive although we did many things that were hard to forgive." Lima paused for a little while before she again began to speak to the listening beings.

"Now that I know your stories, I can see that many of the words that describe your pasts also play a part in the sound of my story. Like you, I am also the only one who managed to survive and bring the story to this place. My previous planet in many ways fell victim to the same weaknesses that your planets did. And therefore I don't think it will come as a surprise to you when I tell you how it all ended after 13 nights of merciless chaos. How the magical being that was my planet ended up dying. And how all the small beings that lived on her disappeared with her demise, although they had fought to prevent it. Because many, many of them had. For a long time, these many beings had realised the consequences of the selfishness of a few, and for a long time they had fought with all their might to solve the crisis in time.

"While the increasing heat around them caused devastating, deadly disasters of fire, earth, water, and air, they came together to fight the catastrophe while there was still time. While countless of their number were forced to flee to safer places, while the death toll rose steadily, they fought who were still able. While yet ambiguous and half-hearted decisions of improvement were made, strong arguments and convincing speeches were put forth in favour of making wholehearted decisions. While it became increasingly harder to survive, and thirst and hunger continued to spread, help was still to be found among the many who shared what they had. While beings who never acknowledged the gravity of the crisis continued to aggravate it, inspiring acts shone out again and again. While more and more reasons to give up and lose faith were created, beings still looked in each other's eyes and shared their hope.

"And when the planet's being sang its last song and its nature exhaled its last breath, and they had lost, they nevertheless knew deep inside that it had been worth the fight. That she had been worth fighting for."

Orion let the tear run down his cheek while he was still looking up at Lima. She took a deep breath and stepped down from the platform from which so many stories had been shared. Here in The Round Place decisions about arrangements on the luminous planet had been made based on just these stories that each being had brought with it. The beings had been given the possibility to recreate the balance that had previously been destroyed. But, Orion thought to himself, only the possibility. The balance was not secured for them. It was up to themselves to make that happen, and, wonderfully, they had made use of the possibility and fought for the balance of the luminous planet. The powerful energy that issued from this immensely significant choice of acting on the possibility for improvement was clearly felt here in The Round Place, Orion was in no doubt.

Just then, a ray from the sky shone down on each of them and the sun showed its face. The mood among those assembled was unmistakable. They were ready to begin.

26

"What your three stories have in common, Nuki, Matu, and Lima, is that they all revolve around beings making inappropriate use of their planet. The same may be said for the rest of your stories, with the exception of yours, Chunlian. Your story is different, but nonetheless related to the solution to the stories we have discussed." Parshi smiled at Chunlian as he spoke these words, and she nodded in acknowledgement. Then he continued: "Now let us look closer at the problems. The way I see it, three main problems appeared on the previous planets of you three. The first is overconsumption. The second is unequal distribution. And the third we may call 'non-optimal use'. And these three issues are interrelated in many ways. Do you agree?"

The nine participants considered the question, answered with confirmation, and went on listening to Parshi's words. He nodded towards Nuki, Matu, and Lima, who sat at the same round table, and said: "You three have all reflected on possible solutions to these three problems. Now let us go through and discuss them all, and hopefully decide on the best one."

"Overconsumption," Matu began, "sounds so simple to avoid. But that requires an attitude in all of us that can be difficult to achieve. An attitude that appreciates the balance of having exactly what we need. An attitude that does not hunger for owning more than what is necessary and does not let itself be drawn into the many temptations of greed. An attitude that enables us to assess what we actually need, and be content to take only that. Because without this attitude and without gratitude for and accept of the balance, overconsumption on the part of some, and thereby lack for others, will appear."

Terra nodded. "This attitude will probably also help us to understand that the luminous planet, just like ourselves, must be in a state of balance. As we consume its resources to fulfil our needs, we must give to it what it requires in order to fulfil its own needs. As we use its soil, we must care for it and ensure that it remains as precious as it was before we touched it."

"I agree," Raven spoke up in her firm voice. "But how does one make sure that everyone has this attitude if it does not come naturally to them? Without gratitude for the balance and the under-standing of its necessity, inequality will happen. And so, overconsumption leads to the next problem in the story: unequal distribution. Because if only one being that does not value sustainable consumption is allowed to dominate, the seeds of inequality will be sown. And since an attitude cannot be forced upon a being's heart, it is not unrealistic to think that inequality may also arise here. I find it hard to see how we can ensure that the attitude that does not promote overconsumption will dominate here." Raven's look was piercing while the beings around her considered her point. It was Lima who broke the thoughtful silence.

"You are right. It is impossible to force a being to know what is good. The good, as I see it, is what benefits most beings by bringing most balance and joy into their lives. The good is what satisfies the needs of the whole, instead of only one. Therefore, a selfish act that harms or lessens the value of the lives of others can never be good. It would be a negative, so to speak. What do you think should dominate on our planet – the good or the negative?"

"The good, of course," Raven answered curtly.

Lima continued. "But imagine that certain beings have an attitude of negative values. Greed, for example. If we wish to fulfil everyone's needs, ought we not also to fulfil this one, although it requires more than the others?"

Raven considered the point, which now seemed obvious. "Of course, this need of greed cannot be allowed to dominate over the others. The planet must be organised in such a way that everyone's needs for balance are met. How and when the balance is achieved may of course vary from being to being, but much is fundamentally similar for all beings. Yes, it must be this fundamental balance that satisfies most beings and simultaneously ensures the planetary balance that must be the foundation of organising life on the planet. Not the negative need whose fulfilment brings imbalance with it."

"Precisely," Lima answered. "So although some beings may possess, for example, a greedy need, we cannot allow them to pursue it, because that would, in this case, bring with it overconsumption and thereby lessen the well-being of the majority. Thus, even though not all have achieved the attitude that genuinely desires the most good to most beings, life on the planet must be organised according to this attitude. The good must dominate for the benefit of all. Because", Lima said in her firm voice, "the well-being of the whole must be what we strive for."

Sahar thought briefly before she asked: "And the root of the third problem, non-optimal use of the planet. How do we avoid this?" She looked at the three beings whose stories had come alive in this moment. The present wove a colourful path in front of them, constantly approaching the final destination, glowing with excitement on the horizon.

Lima replied: "Without deliberate and holistic decisions about how we are to make use of the planet's resources, it is very likely to result in non-optimal use. We will end up using too much of the planet's resources, wasting resources, or damaging resources. Without decisions made in consideration of the whole, we will inevitably misuse the planet's resources in one way or another."

"Agreed, but surely it requires more than simply having the right attitude in order to avoid that. What practical things must we do to ensure optimal use?" Raven asked.

"There are many practical things we have to do," Matu began. "I would start by suggesting the following: To ensure a responsible use of the planet's resources, our consumption must move in the form of a circle. We have to take from the planet, use, reuse, give back to the planet, nurture, and take again. Thus is must continue, because without this circular consumption, imbalance will set in. So in purely practical terms, we must be careful that what we take from the planet does not upset the planet's balance. Then, we must take care of what we use, and reuse it as long as possible. And when it can no longer be reused, we must not accept that it becomes trash in a useless heap piled up somewhere. No, we must be diligent in giving what we have used back to the planet in a form that does not harm it and that it can use again."

"A sustainable pattern of consumption," Sahar nodded.

"That sounds reasonable," Raven added and looked at Nuki as he began to speak.

"Circular consumption must also be the basis of the proper use of energy. The way I see it, we must use only sources of energy that are renewable. The energy from the sun, from wind, and from water, for example. The optimal and most appropriate way to obtain energy from these sources I do not yet know. So we must work diligently to find the best methods. Much investigation lies ahead of us, but they will certainly be worth the effort. I cannot see any other future than that it is sustainable energy sources that should supply our energy here on the luminous planet."

The other beings nodded in agreement. Including Agua, who had kept silent for a long time. Her mind felt like a wild rush of water moving in many different directions. She longed for an overview over the many points that had been raised, and focused on trying to see it in the confusing waves. She closed her eyes and tried to sense the clarity that she knew she was able to create. Slowly the roaring waters calmed and went still. Then she spoke.

"The future of the luminous planet depends on us. Its forests, fields, rivers, and oceans must thrive, and we must take responsibility for ensuring that they do. We cannot ignore that we play a significant role on this planet, and that what we choose to do will have a great impact on it. Moreover, we have learned that if we are to benefit all it should only be a positive impact.

"From what I understand, we have arrived at the following: We must organise our life on the planet after a law that creates and maintains a balance for the planet and all beings living on it, and let this be the law that is above all else. Should we find ourselves going against it, we must try to understand and accept that those of our desires and opinions that do not support the benefit of the whole, cannot be allowed to dominate. Thus, we must train ourselves in the attitude that wishes the best not just for ourselves, but for all and everyone else. This is by no means easy, so it is very important that we also understand and respect the inner struggle it will cause in some, and not simply think ill of them. We are all on the path and we must help each other move forward.

"And we must let the circular pattern of consumption of the planet's resources be the priority. Because the planetary being must thrive just as we ourselves, healthy consumption is of enormous importance. And finally, I would like to add that understanding nature is essential to accomplishing the things mentioned."

Now Chunlian stood up in her excitement and said with a big smile: "Exactly! I believe that one of the most important solutions to the three problems is to know the planet. When one knows and understands the planet better, one naturally appreciates and respects it and can thereby contribute much better to the solutions we come up with and that you mentioned, Agua."

"But won't it take a long, long time to arrive at any solutions by this way, if, before we can get to know nature better, we need a long period of acquiring knowledge, having various experiences, and developing understanding of many things. Is it not much easier simply to be told what others know about nature and then act on the solutions suggested?" Tahi offered.

Chunlian was eager to answer the question and persuade Tahi that he was wrong in thinking this way – but something in her decided to speak otherwise. She took a breath and tried to understand what Tahi saw within his own perspective. Yes, being simply informed of the existing knowledge and then being able to act on the solutions would indeed be quicker than having to acquire one's own knowledge of nature first-hand. Tahi was right about this. But, Chunlian thought before replying: "In solving problems, acting optimally based on someone else's understanding is nearly impossible."

It was quiet for a short while, before Chunlian continued: "We can be told what to do to create balance on the planet, and we can be told why we ought to do it. But if we do not experience this truth as an inner reality for ourselves, our action will never be optimal because it cannot be whole-hearted. And that is if we even choose to act, which is by no means certain. It is our nature to act only on things that we ourselves find meaningful, and not on those things others tell us are meaningful.

"So I agree with you, Tahi, that it would be far quicker simply to tell those who do not know nature themselves what they are to think and do about it. But in that case, the actions that we wish them to perform will never be done.

"No, I believe that the key to achieving actions that are beneficial to nature is to let us realise for ourselves why they are necessary. And we can only do this by getting to know nature through our own eyes and our own bodies. Of course, in cooperation with others and with help from those who already know it well. But most importantly by ourselves. This is the long-term solution, and the one that is sustainable."

The beings surrounding Chunlian nodded again, but her eyes rested in anticipation on Tahi, who looked thoughtful. He was strong and wise enough not to identify himself with his opinions. He saw them as something that stayed with him for a while, but isolated from who he was. So there was no shame in dismissing and changing them when he encountered others that seemed more true.

"I have changed my mind," he said. "In our place of learning we need to get to know nature in order, hopefully, to attain understanding and appreciation of it. I now realise that this knowledge and understanding needs to arise from inside us. If it is imposed on us from the outside, it will be no use to anybody or anything." He smiled and said: "Yes, I think we agree."

"Very well," Parshi said. "If we all see these solutions as the best possible," he looked around at all the assembled beings, who all radiated a yes, "then let them take effect."

Parshi then laid out a large sheet of paper in a golden hue on one of the round tables, and the nine beings gathered around it. Orion observed the event with a look of deep impression in his eyes. He saw them write down all the things they had agreed on. He heard them discuss and then write out a completely detailed plan for how they were going to begin working towards the intended balance for the planet and all its beings. Finally, one by one they wrote a word at the bottom of the paper with a pen whose letters shone in the sunlight. If one looked closely, the meaning and the story inhabiting each of their names could be deciphered.

But looking closely in order to discover the mood in The Round Place was not necessary in this moment. Because just as beautifully as the sun shone down on the assembled beings, just as brightly they smiled at each other, just as right their decisions felt. The solutions that became the conclusion to Nuki, Matu, and Lima's stories about the planets of their past. The solutions that were going to be their true beginning here on the luminous planet.

27

"Imagine all the darkness of the universe gathered in a compact room. On the walls, stars float like openings of light in the massive blackness. Emptiness fills the entire room, apart from a single point that provides a counterweight of solidity. You."

Orion looked into the eyes of the being Bhoukh and felt himself being drawn into his gaze: Orion saw a cube-like box floating in front of him, hovering in the endless universe. Inexplicably, the box hung in space as if suspended by an invisible string. But around the box was only emptiness. And Orion, the viewer of this vision. Floating nearer, he approached the box that grew bigger and bigger. He saw that there were 2 holes in the sides of the box. Carefully he peered through one of the holes and saw that the inside of the box, just as its surroundings, was an empty space. A space in space. Suddenly he noticed a small being standing in one corner of the room.

The being had large eyes, filled with yearning, but that wasn't the most remarkable. Its body was in an eerie way malformed. The head was unnaturally large in relation to the very small and narrow body. The arms and legs were long and thin and appeared to be so weak that they were at risk of breaking. Its belly was round, but the ribs stood out visibly. It had no hair, only naked and slightly wrinkled skin. It radiated one word whose reality made the viewer want to close their eyes from the horrifying sight forever: Hunger.

Orion discovered that the being stuck a hand out of one of the holes in the room's wall. Something was given to it, but Orion could not see what. It must be a food of some sort because the being ate it with weak, slow movements. Then it sat down on the floor of the room. A peculiar silence prevailed, until the being opened its mouth and sang in a clear, delicate voice:

Hunger can be sung to sleep
But the dawn of peace will not break
A harsh truth is waiting
For the sleeper must always awake
Hunger can be quenched with joy
Recognition, happiness, or food
But if it is never entirely eradicated
The stricken will die in no good
The starving seeks a satiety
That all beings must know
But if distribution is undesired
The goal has no way to glow

Then Orion understood that the being in the floating room was trapped. It was trapped in nothingness with no way out. Inside the room it existed in a state of constant starvation and only survived because something in the universe once in a while fed it with a small scrap of its own satiety. Through the round holes of the room, the being's hunger was always sated, but only for a short while. Whoever kept the being alive did absolutely nothing to add value to the being's existence. To save it or set it free from this misery. Satiety only came to visit briefly, never to stay. Clearly, sharing was undesired. The distribution of empty and full were catastrophic. The imbalance between hunger and satiety made the ideal sharing impossible.

It would require a substantial change if a positive fullness was going to fill up the emptiness – and endure.

Orion, who had moved some distance away from the floating room, could no longer see the being through the holes, but only the room from the outside. Suddenly a bright shade approached the room. Orion saw the starving being's arm appear through one of the holes and the shade hovered around the outstretched hand. Orion guessed that the shade would lay food in the hand of the starving being. But he was wrong. Instead, the shade engulfed the entire floating box and magically made the two holes in the box grow. After a while, the six surfaces of the room were perforated by two holes so large that it would be impossible to keep anything trapped in there. The starving being floated out of the room, and a strong bright light grew around its little body. Once the being was free and full of radiant light, Orion recognised it: It was Bhoukh. Without looking back on the now shrinking room, Bhoukh floated towards something glimmering far away in the universe. Orion smiled, because he was quite sure that he knew the place where Bhoukh was headed.

28

Orion smiled at his reflection in the calm waters of the lake. He had followed the white path, which was no longer unfamiliar to him, and had arrived at the luminous centre of the planet. Orion wondered what might be hidden in the depths of the lake. Although the water was clear as air and pure as snow, it was impossible to see the bottom. Perhaps the lake was infinitely deep.

Orion suddenly remembered that this was the very lake in which Terra had found what he was looking for. Terra had sought the key to open the little box of seeds, and the path he had followed confidently had led him here. Then, the lake had been no bigger than Terra could reach to the bottom with his hand. Perhaps the lake had begun as a single drop. Countless dreams had been turned into drops since then! All the same, it was difficult to imagine that something could evolve from being so simple and so small into something so immensely complex and so large. Orion was sure that most who saw a single drop would doubt that it could ever develop into a lake. But also that most would believe that it was possible once they had seen the lake. So whether or not someone would believe the development or not depended on in what stage of the process they were asked. Suddenly it was clear to Orion how dangerous it was to give up in the beginning of a process, where development was a possibility. How many lost joys giving up could result in. Orion thought that every place could be improved if only their inhabitants did not give up on the goals that were set for the common good. The reflection in the lake smiled back at him.

Suddenly an unfamiliar face appeared behind Orion. He turned around and met the eyes of an unknown being. They were friendly and blue and shone with the weight of experience. Orion sensed that this being had gone through difficult things. Hard times that had left deep scars on the being's soul. At the same time the eyes also held forgiveness. A mildness that made Orion feel at ease. The being had long blond hair and a few strands blew across its face in the breeze. The being pushed the strands of hair back and Orion noticed that its hands were covered in large, ugly scars. The being went to stand by Orion's side and looked out over the lake.

"Do you see wisdom in the lake?" the being asked in a bright, gentle voice.

Orion could not take his eyes off the scarred hands.

"Or do you see wisdom in my hands?"

He looked at the being who gave him a wry smile. She laughed.

"My name is Wirtsch. I know who you are. You are the traveller. The exploring and mysterious. The curious and listening. You are Orion."

Her clear blue eyes shone with intensity before she squinted and peered at him in scrutiny.

"But tell me, Orion, who you *really* are. Those are only the others' descriptions of you, but the words might as well describe myself. It is funny with words, how they are so descriptive and yet at the same time never quite capture the truth. Can you describe a feeling as it is? Explain a thought just as you had thought it? Tell about yourself in words that describe you accurately? I do not think so. In words you can only approach the truth. The same word can describe two completely different things equally well. So there must be something futile in words.

"If one separates them so they stand alone, one discovers how weak they are. For example, think of the word *I*. What does it tell us when it stands alone? Joined with other words it can be of great significance, but the word itself leads us nowhere. *I must. I can. I will. I*? Words are weak. So let us not give them too much power. Of course, words are necessary. Where would we be without words? It makes sense to have them, it does, but what I mean to say is that they are no more than words. I suppose you could say that what I am expressing in words is not my truth. But my thought and my feeling behind the words is. Words are words. Words are not truth."

Silence fell and Orion tried to understand what Wirtsch had said. *Words are not truth.*

"Perhaps words are part of the truth," Orion suggested.

Wirtsch looked at him, surprised. Orion continued. "Do you expect the words to *become* what they describe in order to be true? That words attempt to describe the truth tells us something. Perhaps they do not precisely capture the truth if it is a feeling or a thought or a mood they are trying to describe. It is impossible for them to precisely describe a feeling, for example, because they *are* not the feeling. Just because words are only capable of describing the feeling does not make them untrue. It just doesn't make them perfect. But is anything perfect?

"You asked me who I really am. And I know that I am certainly not perfect either. But I am always on the way. I seek truth because I seek understanding. I seek understanding because I seek development. And I seek development because I seek a final goal. Using words, I write about thoughts, my experiences, and my understandings. To reach my goal I would not be without words.

"I journeyed to your luminous planet in order to reach my innermost goal. I do not yet know what that is, but I am certain that the achievement of the goal I seek exists somewhere in the future. Every step brings me further along my path. Perhaps the goal is far away, perhaps near. Perhaps I will only know what it is the moment I reach it."

Orion smiled and they sat in silence for a while. They had sat down on the white path and were admiring the beautiful calm lake. Orion once again thought about the evolution of the lake and its transformation from one single drop to infinitely many. Wirtsch interrupted his thoughts and said: "I did not always live on this wonderful planet." She fell silent again, her eyes fixed on the beauty of the lake.

Orion looked at her carefully and noticed that she was moving her hands nervously. The scars danced on her skin. Wirtsch continued in a serious voice: "I used to live on a planet very far from this one. But many things happened that made me ... that I had to leave it. You see, Orion, on my previous planet I lived a life that is almost not worth talking about. I owned nothing and was therefore labelled as nothing. I lived a miserable life with no substance.

"In order to survive it was necessary for the planet's inhabitants to be employed. That was the only way to be rewarded with the tickets that gave access to all the things required for survival. I had never had the opportunity to enter employment and therefore I was left to the harsh reality of nothingness.

"Every single day I debated with myself whether I should continue my life or give myself the pleasure of ending it. I desired the latter, but something in me denied my desire, and so I carried on in my meaningless struggle of an existence."

"Why did you have to be employed in order to obtain these tickets?" Orion asked.

Wirtsch shrugged and replied: "Fairness, my friend. And it does make sense in principle. One has to strive for happiness. It doesn't just float in and land on top of your head by itself. You have to work for it. But the problem is that not everyone is the same. Everyone does not possess the same opportunities and strengths. And I did not have the opportunity to work for my happiness. There was no place that needed me. I was left to my own misfortune. I didn't receive any tickets, and soon I had lost hope that I ever would.

"But one day a door opened for me. A door of opportunity and happiness. There finally was a place that needed my labour. It only rewarded 8 tickets per day, but for me it was better than nothing at all."

Orion interrupted again: "What did you have to do at this place?"

Wirtsch clenched her hands and closed her eyes tightly as if trying to repress something. She glanced quickly at Orion before answering: "I dug pits."

"You dug pits?" Orion asked. He could see that Wirtsch was ashamed.

"Yes. A distance below the planet's surface there was a layer of coloured balls that were very valuable. The more balls, the more tickets. And the deeper one dug, the darker the colour of the balls. The more tickets they were worth. The darkest was a deep crimson, the most valuable of all. I worked every day to dig pits so other workers could collect the balls from the ground.

"I began to receive more and more tickets because the pits I dug contained balls in valuable colours. I also began to work longer hours because I felt a constant need to receive more and more tickets. I felt better because now that I had more tickets, I had access to more resources. I had access to more things and to a place to live. I worked hard, and ..." Wirtsch fell silent. She looked down at her worn-out hands and sighed.

"I suppose I had greater outer wealth. But inside me I was exactly as miserable as before. Because I discovered how important the balls were. Not for me and for my place of work, but for the planet. The balls created balance in the planet's system, so when we removed them from the earth every day we were causing a huge imbalance. I was participating in destroying my own planet. The sense of guilt grew alongside the pressure that made me continue the work."

"What pressure?" Orion asked indignantly. Why would anyone carry on doing something they knew was wrong?

"Pressure from everyone around me. The value of the coloured balls made people selfish. Everyone wanted to get the balls and they depended on me. That's why they pressured me to work harder and more, and before I knew it my life consisted of digging pits. I spent all my time on it. But I don't want to only blame the people around me. There was also a pressure from myself. Because I knew what a terrible fate awaited me if I stopped working. I would no longer receive tickets and I would lose everything I owned."

Wirtsch glanced at Orion who was looking sadly at the beautiful radiant lake before them. She smiled.

"I know that I acted selfishly too, Orion. But it wasn't going to continue. As if struck by lightning, I awoke one day with an indescribable sense of clarity. A question gripped me and impatiently demanded an answer: *Does the growth of ticket wealth constitute happiness?* I knew the answer right away."

Now Wirtsch was also looking at the lake and its incredible radiance.

"It was as if I had until that point been trying to expand the lake of my happiness. I had struggled to make it greater and I was willing to do anything to make it happen. I had fed the lake with my time, my body, my values, and sadly also with the planet's resources.

"Sure enough, my lake did grow, but I was expanding it using indefensible drops. Do you understand what I mean, Orion? If the lake of my happiness is to grow, the crucial factor is *how* I let this happen. Is it at the cost of others and of myself? Or is it using means that are responsible and decent? Sustainable and beneficial to all? Because it must be that way. I realised that happiness must be achieved fairly. A drop has to increase if it is to become a lake. But the most important thing is that it happens with responsibility and fairness to its surroundings and surroundding beings."

Wirtsch looked at Orion and their eyes met again. Orion noticed that her blue eyes looked like a smaller but completely identical version of the radiant lake. He was so grateful for the words she had shared with him. He admired her insight into fairness and her ability to admit her own mistakes. Admitting one's own mistakes and accepting that one has committed them had to be some of the most important abilities in the development of the self, Orion thought.

"Thank you," he said.

Wirtsch smiled at Orion. Then she asked: "What for, my friend? I have been sitting here talking in words, but are they even true?" Orion looked at her, puzzled. She grinned at him, and they both began to laugh.

29

Orion broke through the lake's surface and now floated in its ice-cold water. He was sure that the passage of time had stopped, because countless thoughts flew through his head while the rushing of the water following his fall still roared in his ears. Orion sensed that he was the centre of the lake, like a pupil in a round eye.

At first, the water flowed gently around him, forming a perfect circle. Orion's eyes followed the current and he discovered that it moved in sync with his gaze. Evidently, his being had an influence on the ring of water around him. He wondered why it was suddenly beginning to rush around so fast. A circle so agitated, Orion thought. He would never have guessed that below the peaceful surface of the lake such a state of unrest and confusion would exist. Was it always so? It was as if the drops of the lake had separated themselves from each other and no longer acted as a whole. They had become an infinite number of individuals that lived their own selfish lives, independent of the unity of the lake. It seemed impossible, but it was the truth. The hopeless truth.

The drops were now rushing around Orion even faster and he lost control of himself. Now Orion wished more than anything else that the chaotic current would stop. He desired balance and harmony in the disrupted drops.

The drops hurled him in different directions and made him dizzy. The only thing that Orion was still in control of was his own inner self. Who he really was, he thought to himself, while his body was tossed around in the centre of the lake.

If his being really had the power to influence the rushing ring of drops, he wanted to grant it peace and balance. Because right now, the water that heaved around him was not a circle. A circle is continuous. It is complete. And as long as the drops acted as selfish individuals, they could never form a circle.

Orion intensely desired to chance this situation. And he knew that only he could bring about the change. Despite the unrest he was nonetheless the centre of the lake. He was its central point, and if the belief in action should not begin there, where else? Orion closed his eyes and imagined a circle shining with peace. Balance and harmony. Drops united in a perfect sea.

Orion opened his eyes and was slowly carried to the surface of the lake by gentle waves. The roaring waters around him had stilled. So had the wild current.

Orion floated peacefully in the centre of the perfect circle that he had caused to be, and he felt like a drop that was part of a coherent ocean.

30

Cold and heat never agree. Yet at the same time they always mirror each other. Because without the existence of the other they do not exist. They cannot be described in isolation but depend on their opposite in order to be explained. Therefore, they often ask each other whether they can truly be called opposites and not simply brother and sister, different but also alike.

Orion shivered. He had fallen into the planet's luminous centre, the lake. Now he stood on the path of white stones that surrounded the lake and was filled with a peculiar feeling of being hot and cold at the same time. His body was wet and chilled to the core from the bright water of the lake. But his mind was warm and shone with a wonderful clarity. He felt the extremes of heat and cold at the same time, and the sum of the two generated an incredible energy in Orion. Without giving it any particular thought, Orion began to run and sprinted around the lake. He followed the white path along the clear water until his feet turned where the path split in two. Orion ran faster and faster. The flowers and trees that grew on either side of the path he passed so quickly that he barely noticed them. He wondered if he had ever run before, and carried on although the answer was no.

Soon Orion had run across all the stones of the planet's white path, and he came to an abrupt halt.

A large white object rushed towards him. Orion covered his eyes. He was sure that it would crash into him, but when he looked again, the white object had stopped right in front of him. Orion calmed his rapidly beating heart and walked to the other side of the object. Now he noticed that it had windows and doors. Orion suddenly recalled that he had once seen a similar object, far in the distance, when he had just arrived on the luminous planet. It moved along a path that began somewhere unknown far away and terminated here in the planet's luminous centre.

Orion peered through one of the windows and saw a small being that stood up in the same instant. It exited the white object, laid a hand on it, and muttered a quiet 'thank you'. It did not seem to have noticed Orion who with his head tilted to the side was wondering why the being had said thank you. Orion took a step closer and gasped when the being suddenly spoke: "Contact. Be grateful for the contact, Orion."

The being turned around and curiously observed Orion's confused look. "Paths that lead us through life are valuable. Paths that lead the way and lead to goals. Paths that lead out of isolation and loneliness." The being gently laid its other hand on the large object, which emitted a short melody and departed.

"Paths – that create contact?" Orion asked and tried to understand what the other being was getting at. He looked it in the eyes and asked: "Who are you?"

"I am Ino."

"What path do you come from?" Orion asked.

Ino smiled. "Come," she said and continued down the path that would soon lead Orion to answers.

31

A world of bubbles. Isolated bubbles. Ino's planet existed in 9 layers. On the planet itself, wealthy beings lived in excellent conditions. The possibilities for connection with other beings and experiences on the planet were ideal. The planet's busy beings easily moved between the places they desired to be because the transport between them worked flawlessly. And yet, they spent most of their time in complaining and accusations. Because above them hung eight layers of bubbles that cast shadows on the planet's beings. For every layer the distance between the bubbles increased, thus isolating the individual bubbles more and more.

The bubbles were not empty. They contained other living beings, haunted by misery and sorrow. These beings lived each in their own floating bubble and were cut off from their surroundings. They all shared the same desperate desire: to break through the wall of their bubble and be able to contact the life they knew existed on the surface of the planet. They looked down on the planet's beings and always asked themselves why they in particular had been left to this lonely fate. The worst and most unbearable was the emptiness that grew inside them day by day. It felt as if it ate up the isolated ones from the inside. An emptiness that filled everything. They longed intensely to break out of the bubble and embrace the life to which they were merely spectators.

Through her own bubble, Ino had watched many isolated ones go mad with longing. It had begun as a dream of a better life. A frustration with the injustice of it. Then it developed into aggressive movements and actions in the confining floating bubbles. Probably also terrifying cries and words, Ino thought, though she did not know for certain. Because she could not hear any outside sound through the wall of her own bubble.

It happened more and more often that bubbles burst, and the lonely and now lifeless beings slowly descended towards the planet's surface. The only impact the being would ever have was the small speck of sorrow that it left on the perfect ground. The isolation clearly became increasingly unbearable, Ino was sure of this.

One day, her own feeling of emptiness was mixed with something unknown. Perhaps an idea. Ino hesitated. She suddenly had a sense that she would be able to break out of her bubble and make contact with the world she dreamed of. Faith had penetrated the wall of the bubble and made its way into her mind. And now it was Ino's turn to break out. She used her faith to push the bubble into a path that would lead her towards a new and unknown planet. Through the bubble's walls Ino looked back at her previous planet. She knew she was doing the right thing. She turned around and was met by a light so bright that she had *to cover her eyes. She followed the path of light. A bubble floating in the universe. A bubble bursting and becoming one with the air around it.*

Ino breathed in the fresh air. She smiled. The luminous planet had gained a new inhabitant.

32

The grain in the field danced before Orion, but he did not notice its beauty. He was filled with anxiety and doubt and had therefore retraced his steps to a familiar place. The field where he had encountered Pheko and Terra a little while ago, was the first place that came to mind when he felt the need for safety. Orion hoped that the place would cure the growing sense of unease, but the constantly moving grain only made matters worse.

It was shortly after he had taken leave of Ino that a sudden inner discomfort had arisen within him. His thoughts were painted dark and his emotions infected each other with sorrow.

While he sat in the field and became more and more irritated with himself, he caused doubt to appear in his mind. Was it even right to be here? He missed his star, and he felt that his arguments in favour of leaving it had been lacking. He felt profoundly lonely, although he had now made the acquaintance of more living beings than he had ever known before. Because it felt as if he was so very different from all those he had met. The beings of the luminous planet had all found their path and reached their goal. It made Orion doubt where his own path was leading him. And if he was even on the right path.

Orion held back a tear. Did the truth he wanted to find even exist? And if it did, and if he found it, what would he do with it? What if he would still be unsure of his goal and his path then? Orion sighed in frustration. He supposed that in the end, it didn't really matter whether the truth would help him find his path or not. After all, he was only a minuscule piece of the universe, and there would still be so many other pieces who did not know the truth and had not found their own place either. Because this luminous planet was only one of seventeen other planets. Planets that had either not realised the light of truth, or had ignored or fought against it. And as long as there were forces that fought against the light, would it even be possible to create one infinite truth for all?

Orion felt so helpless and small. He was almost entirely convinced that he had no power to make a difference in the vast universe.

Sadly, Orion picked a head of grain and began to pick it apart.

"A piece in a game," he sighed.

Behind him, a calm voice spoke: "Who?"

Orion answered without looking up. A tear rolled down his cheek, and joined the remains of the grain Orion had picked apart.

"The grain. The beings. Perhaps the entire universe. I don't know," he replied miserably.

The voice behind Orion took shape, and he saw that it was a small, charming being with dark hair and warm eyes. It beamed happily at Orion and squatted down in front of him.

"You look sad," the being said.

"If only you could help me," Orion sighed.

"I can. But you have to catch 3 of my words." The being stood up again and set off at a run across the field.

Orion stared after it, confused. Curious as always, he got up and sprang after the little being.

"Wait!" he called, breathing hard.

The being looked back over her shoulder, caught sight of Orion and called back: "Doubt!"

"It fills everything," Orion shouted back.

They continued to run.

"Existence!"

"An unanswerable question," Orion replied breathlessly.

He did not understand what the unfamiliar being was trying to do. But she sped up, and Orion followed through the seemingly endless field of grain.

"Well-being."

Orion stopped. He looked perplexed at the being, who also stopped and looked back at Orion.

"What do you mean?" he asked.

"The doubt about existence affects your well-being, Orion."

He looked sceptically at the smiling being, who continued with a suddenly serious voice: "I have felt the same way myself. *Don't think so much, Odimma,*

152

it doesn't matter, they all said to me. But how could I take life seriously when I did not even know why I was living it?" She fell silent and looked at Orion.

He had lain down in the field and stared up into the sky, his eyes empty.

Odimma went on: "Little by little life lost its meaning for me. Everything became pointless. There was not a single being on my planet who could tell me why we lived, and why we might not just as well not live. I couldn't find an answer within myself either. So I concluded that life on my planet was like a play, in which some played the leading parts, others struggled to secure a role, and others again would never be more than spectators in the audience. A greedy director controlled the whole show and rarely shared his profits with others than himself and a select few. My planet was one big comedy, and I did not want to play a part."

"Then what did you do?" Orion asked.

"At first I tried to persuade the others that they would have to come down from the stage and look up. To find out where they were going. And ask themselves *why* they were going at all. Throw away the script and consider why they obediently followed it all the way through life. What if it did not tell the truth? Manipulated or didn't make sense? That's when obedience and trust become very dangerous."

Orion saw the frustration in Odimma's eyes. He asked: "But they did not listen to you?"

"They had been brainwashed by their script lines. No new idea could penetrate their barricaded thoughts. I don't know if that was the reason for the outbreak of the epidemic or if something else caused it. In any case, the planet was struck by a deadly disease that spread throughout the population in the blink of an eye. The consequences of the disease were different for every participant of the play. Some beings were innocent, and I found it terribly unjust that they had to suffer because of the faults of others. But it was clear that others were hit by the epidemic as a lesson for their life's actions. Or rather, their lack of action.

"The bodies of some beings shrunk. They became thinner and shorter and lost their voice. Their eyes revealed that they had reached the size that corresponded to the effort and the influence they had exerted on the planet.

"Others lost their hair and sprouted huge boils all over the body. They tried to conceal their hideous appearance behind blankets, but I knew that this was not the first time they hid themselves. They had lived in constant fear of the director's reaction to their strength. They had kept silent and hidden behind his commands and wasted their inner resources.

"And finally, there were those whose symptoms were almost the worst. Some of their body parts grew completely out of proportion. One being's mouth enlarged constantly. It grew larger than the rest of the body, until eventually the lips hung down below the being's shoulders. The voice became so loud and shrill that everyone avoided the monstrous being who through its entire life selfishly had promoted its own interests at the expense of others."

Orion shivered, but Odimma continued her tale.

"I was the only being on my planet who was not hit by the epidemic. In a short while the play had turned into a tragedy.

"All around me, sick and insane beings swarmed around, purposeless and full of doubt. Yes, now doubt had taken root inside them, and they were struggling to cope with the intolerable feeling. *Why are we a part of this play?* I heard them scream. *How will it end? Does it have any meaning?,* other beings asked in frustration.

"For my part, I knew that my ending was not going to play out here. I had to leave them. I had to start over someplace where I could see a meaning in life. I decided to leave my planet. And although I carried the doubt with me, I was also filled with a hope that meaning had to exist somewhere in the universe. I still did not have an answer to the question of why everything, the entire existence of the universe, should be better than nothing, no universe at all. But a new thought grew within me, one that was positive towards the existence of everything: Why should such a complex and intelligent universe exist if there was no meaning in it? What kind of force would waste such tremendous amounts of energy in creation if it was entirely unnecessary and meaningless? And how could I think that a being like me, so small compared to the enormous, perhaps infinite universe, could really figure out what its meaning was?

"I have never found answers to these questions. But an answer has found me. I must live my life in the faith that there are forces and energies that are greater than me that possess answers and meaning. I have to trust that I cannot understand everything myself. And then not always live my life from the vast, incomprehensible perspective of the universe, but from the perspective that fits me. When I zoomed in on my own perspective, I realised that it is the only place from which I can thrive and create well-being for myself and others. For all of us, whom I believe form a meaningful whole.

33

Orion smiled at Odimma.

"Thank you," he said.

She tilted her head. Orion continued: "You really *could* help me."

"Did you catch my words?" Odimma asked.

Orion smiled again. "Every one of them."

For a while they sat in silence in the field. Orion closed his eyes, and an image appeared in his mind:

A deep blue sky covered with stars. Beings in all the hues of the rainbow danced on the stars. Some jumped from one star to another. Laughter. Amid all the beauty, Orion suddenly noticed that some of the stars were falling out of the sky. More and more. Orion watched a star on which a joyful being danced. Suddenly a string was attached to the star, and it was as if something pulled at it. The being fell, plummeting into nothingness. Orion did not let the string attached to the star out of sight. At the end of the string stood a being on a small planet, struggling to pull the star towards itself. The being firmly grasped the string, and when the star came close to the planet, the being handily swept the star into a dark sack standing by its side. Thus it continued. More and more stars were stolen from the sky, and the colourful dancing beings disappeared.

Orion shivered and opened his eyes. He looked in front of him and his eyes opened wide in surprise as he noticed a large black sack standing before him.

"At least I'm curious to see what is hiding inside it."

Orion could hear that it was not Odimma's voice speaking. He looked slightly baffled at the unfamiliar being who sat precisely where Odimma had been just a brief moment ago.

"Well, if you won't look, I will," the being said.

"But where did you come from?" Orion asked.

"I wonder which of the two of us is the more curious. Something tells me that I am. But one never knows. Neither can one know what is hidden in a sack unless one looks inside."

Orion began to get annoyed. "Where is Odimma?" he asked.

"Inside the sack, perhaps?" the being replied, smiling.

"Look here," Orion began, his irritation growing. But the other being interrupted him.

"I know what you are going to say. And what you are going to ask after that. But if you want to discover who I am and what my past is, you will have to complete the vision that has appeared in your mind. This is the dark sack that you saw, and I am the being Pea who once greedily stole the 16 stars. And before you turn your eyes to the sack once more, I bid you remember one thing: Peace is always possible."

158

Orion looked at Pea, who smiled back at him. She nodded towards the sack, and Orion stood up and peered carefully into it. Without being able to help himself, he suddenly tumbled forwards and fell into the dark deep of the sack.

34

Pea smiled at the bright stars of the night. Sixteen lights in the sky that always brought her joy. Right now, they shone brighter than ever before. She sat down on the planet's hard surface and dreamed herself far away. Dreamed herself away to the shining stars where she was certain that happiness existed.

Every night she ran to the highest point of the planet and jumped towards the stars. She desperately wanted to reach them and their golden riches of light and warmth. But every night she fell asleep with her eyes wet with tears, still lacking for stars as much as the night before.

One night, Pea caught sight of something that at first delighted her, but soon after filled her with overpowering jealousy. The sixteen stars that she knew so well were suddenly inhabited by unfamiliar beings. They danced and jumped around on the mighty stars, waving down to Pea on her little planet. She waved back at them miserably and entered her dreamland with one anxious question: Was this fair?

Pea sensed a strange feeling grow inside her. She felt let down. Had she not always dreamed of a life with the stars? Why, then, had this wish not been fulfilled for her, but for those other beings, who probably did not even love the stars nearly as much as Pea did? Now she was condemned to a life of jealousy on her little planet, which immediately felt infinitely distant from the stars.

Sweat ran down her face, but Pea did not let go. The string tore at her hands and blood dripped on the surface of the planet.

"For the stars!" Pea yelled and tugged with all her might.

She toppled backwards, still clinging to the string. She let out a sigh of relief and stood up to take a look inside the sack. Pea beamed with pride and looked admiringly at the bright star that now belonged to her alone.

"Help me!" a shrill voice cried. In the sky a homeless being floated, staring at Pea, its eyes full of need. It was the being that had occupied the star and for so long had prevented Pea from possessing it. She looked coldly at the being before she whispered: "You should be ashamed. You occupy something as if it were your own, and then demand help from the rightful owner. No, you'll have to pay with the emptiness that for far too long has been the lot of an innocent like me. And tell me, you miserable thief, why I should ever want to help my enemy."

The being became smaller and smaller and was now floating so far away that Pea could no longer see it, and therefore no longer needed to care about it.

Pea sat on top of her sack that contained the sixteen stars.

161

"I am happy," she repeated to herself.

If only she said it enough times, perhaps the words would become true. She looked away from the brightness of the stars and into the night sky. It was pitch black. It looked at once immensely large and infinitely small. Pea could not tell if it was located far, far from her, or if it enveloped her and she herself was in the middle of it. The black sky was both empty and full. Pea knew that this could not be so, but she did not know which of the two opposites was true. Because there was no perspective in the sky. There was not a single light that could tell Pea anything about the night sky. There was not a single star. There was only this unending blackness existing all around her, or not existing anywhere. Pea felt like she was losing her mind over the uncertainty. But most of all, she was lonely.

"I am happy," she said again.

In her head she could still hear the screams and cries for help of the dancing beings. They called to her, begging her for mercy. *Please don't steal our homes. How will this benefit you?* Pea covered her ears. She knew what the next voice would scream: *End this remorseless war.* A tear fell from Pea's cheek and the salty drop stung as it hit her bloody hand. She had started a war.

But she had been victorious. She owned all the stars of the night and her greatest wish had been fulfilled. She had destroyed the greedy beings that had mocked her for so long. But another part of her said that this was not the feeling of victory. And besides, the stars had lost most of their brightness. Only a few of the stars in the sack still shone. Pea refused to admit it, but deep within herself she knew that she had loved the night stars more when they belonged to the night. She took no pleasure in them now that they were inside the sack.

She shook her head and tried to push away the uncomfortable thought. She was too proud to admit her mistake. And if she did, what could she do about it? The sky was empty, the beings were gone, and the stars were dying. Before long, she would be the last living being in existence, and then it would not matter what was right and what was wrong.

But the doubt never left Pea. Rather, it was busy making preparations for a war that would take place inside her. A war whose outcome would decide her fate.

35

Orion landed in the field with a bump. The black sack was gone, but Pea was still sitting by his side. He looked at her with suspicion.

"Peace is always possible," Pea repeated.

Orion took a deep breath. A part of him understood why she had acted the way she did. And yet he knew that her greed had led her towards evil. Unjust choices she had made, seen from the perspective of the stars and the other beings.

"You caused a war," Orion said sadly.

"Yes, the war was my fault. I destroyed my surroundings. But the worst of it is that I did it although a small part of myself knew that it was wrong. Once I truly realised that I had acted selfishly, a great need for forgiveness arose within me. But there was nobody but myself left to grant it to me. I was alone, and yet the war was still not ended. As I said, I had destroyed everything around me. At first, I thought that meant that I had won. But once the feeling of shame appeared, an even longer and tougher war began. I was fighting against myself. The evil that for so long had been dominating within me was suddenly challenged by something good and bright that also resided inside."

"I'm guessing that the good was victorious in the end?" Orion interrupted.

"Eventually, yes. It is hard to explain how it happened. It felt as if the easiest thing would be to let the darkness within me win. It was so powerful and clever. I knew that I could persuade myself that what I had done was the right thing. That the stars belonged to me and nobody else. I knew that I could live the rest of my life in this imaginary happiness and pride if only I allowed myself to do so. If I poisoned the good that was trying to gain a foothold in me. If only I suppressed it and killed it off. Letting the selfishness in me win would be the easiest option."

"But not the best?" Orion asked.

Pea thought for a moment before answering. "The selfish and greedy filled most of me. But the loving, forgiving, and peaceful, despite its minuscule size, was nevertheless incredibly powerful. Every time I paid it a little bit of attention, it grew rapidly, transforming great parts of its opposite into light. And at the same time, it convinced my mind that the good possessed the more important values. I could hear it speaking to me with a voice that struck my entire being. Everywhere I could sense its words of wisdom that gently but powerfully said: *Peace is always possible.*"

Orion smiled at Pea, and her eyes shone with peace. They sat in silence for a while, until Orion asked: "What about your stars?"

"The stars never did and never will belong to me. Once I realised this truth, I was filled with great sorrow and pain. Because in that moment I realised that I had made an evil mistake. One of the hardest things is to forgive oneself. Especially when you are convinced that you do not deserve it. But the bright voice inside me said that forgiving my own evil actions was the only key to the gate into a brighter future. So I forgave myself. I forgave myself until I finally accepted my own forgiveness. And in that moment, I knew that there was hope of making amends for my actions. I set the stars free from the dark sack, and they floated happily back towards the sky."

"And you never lacked for stars since then?" Orion asked.

"I felt richer than ever! Because the light of the stars lived within me. They led me towards a future where I could make sure that another war like that would never happen again. That's why I journeyed to this luminous planet. To the place where peace will always prevail."

36

Orion was making his way out of the little valley where he had spent so much time. He looked over his shoulder and smiled at all the happy life that resided there. He was filled with experiences and needed to think through his thoughts. Orion did not know where his feet were taking him but he followed them trustingly. They stepped up the slope of the hill past peaceful flowers in the most beautiful colours. Then they came to an abrupt halt. Orion looked up and for the second time was overwhelmed by the magnificence of the great tree. It was the same tree that Orion had seen back when he was newly arrived on the luminous planet. He smiled at the tall tree with the mighty crown and rejoiced at how much he had learned since their last meeting. Like the previous time, he laid his hand on the trunk of the tree. A sudden gust of wind stirred up a whirl of leaves around Orion. His vision was veiled for a moment, and then a clear image was born in Orion's mind:

A light shone down on him, so bright that Orion had to close his eyes. He sensed that the bright light came from the crown of the tree. Orion discovered that the ground surrounding the great tree was shaking and moving. Frightened, Orion pressed himself against the tree trunk and saw the mysterious movements drum up a cloud of brown earth around him. He could not determine if the phenomenon was merely something he imagined, or if it was really taking place in reality. The light above him shone brighter than ever and interrupted to Orion's doubt.

Just then, a loud creaking came from the tree, and it was torn clean out of the ground. Orion was paralysed with fear. The tree began to float, or the ground below it was lowered. It was impossible to tell. Clinging to one of the tree's roots, Orion hung in the air, surrounded by a ring of earth. Within moments, everything else had disappeared, and the only thing remaining in the vast universe was the mighty tree and Orion's small being, surrounded by a circle of whirling earth. Nothingness filled everything around them.

Then a familiar light shone down on Orion once more. It was the light whose source had come from the tree's crown just moments before. Orion squinted towards the source of the light and tried to bring it into focus. Yes, it did indeed come from the treetop. Orion wanted to reach it. Something told him that it was important that he identified this desire. While he and the tree were still surrounded by the swirling ring of earth, Orion started to climb up towards the tree's crown.

Sweat ran down his face. His arms burned with the effort, and blood ran from scratches in his hands and feet. Orion gasped as the branch he was holding on to snapped. He tumbled into nothingness at infinite speed. At the last moment, he grabbed hold of the root of the tree, the same that he had clung to at the beginning of the climb. He would have to start over. The earth circle whirled closer to Orion now, and hard clumps of soil struck his body. He knew that he had to hurry. He looked up into the crown of the tree; it seemed so far away from him. Giving up was so tempting.

Orion gritted his teeth and took another path. He reached for the largest branches and moved faster and faster towards the top of the tree. The light grew brighter. He sensed the ring of earth expanding, making room for him to move. Orion was filled with hope and climbed yet higher, up through the countless green leaves in the crown. It was as if he in that moment became aware of his own strength. As if he became stronger the higher he climbed. The light was just above him.

Orion breathed in the fresh air as he stuck his head through the top of the tree crown. His jaw dropped in delight at the incredible sight that met him; colours, sounds, and fragrances blended all around him. It felt as if all the joy, wisdom, and love that Orion had ever experienced in life was concentrated in this very location.

But he was not surprised. Because the wonderful surroundings perfectly corresponded to his inner state at the moment. Inexplicably, they were one and the same. He had not only climbed up the tree

169

towards the light. He had climbed towards his own inner light. Orion took in the glittering, vibrant colours. Colours that began to take shape as fire, air, water, and earth. They moved towards each other until they formed a perfect circle around Orion. He understood.

37

Parshi picked another white flower while he listened patiently to Orion's words. A full bouquet. They were sitting on the bench beneath the tree, near The Final Place. During Orion's tale, Parshi sometimes responded with "Interesting," or "I understand," while nodding encouragingly.

"I journeyed here, to the luminous planet, in a search for truth," said Orion. "I am not sure which truth I was seeking, but I was certain that I would find it here. That it was hidden somewhere in the light. That it was a truth that created the radiance that surrounds the planet. And I am sure that you have all been part of creating this radiance. You have fought and prevailed against evil. The abandoned and empty planets that I had seen through the window in my star were the scars of your past battles. But from the empty planets, you brought with you a bright hope that you planted here on the luminous planet.

"Until now, I thought that you would also bring this light to me. But none of you have.

"A little while ago I was overcome with great sorrow and doubt. Hopelessness. A dark question about our very existence. But Odimma's faith in the meaning of the whole restored the hope in me. Like Odimma, you have all contributed to showing me the path. You did not show me or tell me about the goal at the end of the path but have guided and inspired me towards it. And I began to understand that none of you *could* show me the goal, even if you wanted to."

"What do you mean?" Parshi asked and looked at Orion, puzzled.

"You cannot bring me a goal that you have not yet reached yourselves. And you will never reach that goal until you embrace the fact that the outer world is simply a reflection of our inner worlds.

"Ever since I arrived on the luminous planet, mysterious images have been appearing to me. I am still not certain if they have taken place physically as well." Orion paused for a moment. He looked out over the bright centre of the luminous planet, listening to its happy voices. He took a deep breath before continuing: "The images I have seen are about circles. The first time it was in the form of fiery flames that approached each other. They were like two half-circles that could not complete themselves. The second time it happened on the way up the countless stairs in the strong wind. The stairs were rotating and suddenly became a spinning circle around me. There was a hole in it. The third time, in the lake as a wild current of selfish drops of water. They were not acting as a whole body of water, and therefore could not form a circle. The fourth time was at the exit of the planet's centre near the great tree on the hilltop. An angry ring of earth. Whirling restless and incoherent and therefore also incomplete. It is as if these four images have been trying to tell me something about *wholeness*." Orion looked at Parshi.

"Have you seen other images, Orion?" he asked.

Orion eyes lit up before he answered: "Yes, there is another image. When I was at the tree, I saw a powerful, bright light, and I climbed up to reach it. It was difficult and harder than anything I have ever done. But eventually I reached the crown of the tree and looked out from the top. Up there was the warmest light I have known, like pure joy in its simplest form. But there was something else, too. Fire, air, water, and earth formed a great circle around me. It was perfect."

Parshi picked one final white flower before quietly announcing that the bouquet was now complete.

"Suddenly I understood the images that had been appearing to me. The fire, wind, water, and earth had formed incoherent circles that only *I* could complete. In order to complete them, I had to realise that I, like everything else, was part of them. That we are all part of the same whole. As soon as I realised this, the circles became perfect. But I only understood this once I turned my awareness on myself.

"And now I know that this is the realisation you need to attain if you are to reach your goals *completely*. All seventeen of you have contributed to the planet's wonderful radiance. But you have only reached the seventeen goals *around* ourselves.

Observing from afar, I, too, believed that the attainment of the seventeen goals in the planet's outer world would suffice to perfect the luminous planet. But I was wrong. An 18th goal must be reached."

Parshi sat with a questioning expression. Orion thought for a few moments. Then he spoke with a voice at once powerful and fragile: "This final goal must be achieved before the luminous planet can shine with all its power. But, actually, I think it is not the final goal at all, but the very first. The most important and universal. Because this eighteenth goal resides in the fulfilment of all the other seventeen and is the very source that enables and ensures their continual fulfilment. The eighteenth goal is a truth that must be realised.

"And now I know that this is the truth I have been seeking for all this time. And now, just now, the truth shines clearly before me. The truth smiles at me from the magical face of the eighteenth goal, and its words radiate this: The outer world is a reflection of the inner worlds of us beings. Our thoughts, feelings, and ideas of goodwill appear as positives around us. And reversely, our weaknesses appear as negatives and will forever bring ensuing disaster while their source remains vital – while weakness still lives in us.

"The creation of problems in the outer world and the opposite, their solutions, thus originate in ourselves. Everything depends on whether we change the negative aspects in ourselves into positives.

174

Whether we let the positives flourish. Until our weaknesses are realised and changed, their consequences in the world around us can and will continue to exist, dominate, and expand.

"This is why you have not yet fully achieved the seventeen goals. Because you have been missing the conscious realisation that the solution to your problems resides just as much within yourselves as in the world around you. Because in the world around you, you have managed to solve the problems. You have put an end to poverty and hunger. You have stopped war and injustice. You have ended all the countless ways in which nature can be abused. But it is very likely that the attainment of these goals is only temporary. Because if the weaknesses that originally caused the disasters on your previous planets still remain within you, the same disaster may as well appear here. If you truly desire to reach the seventeen goals that each of you has been fighting for, you must open the door to everything that resides within you. You must shine a light into the inner room of your weaknesses and try to understand them. To accept their existence, until one day you make the choice to open a window and set them free and let their opposite strengths take their place.

"Because each of the seventeen weaknesses that previously caused their own disaster on your previous planets, have an opposite strength. Each of the negative aspects within our nature can be changed to a positive. Selfishness to generosity. Fear to courage. Deceit to honesty. Hatred to charity. Narrow-mindedness to holism. And so on. Always we have a choice to let either the good or the negative side reign and thus develop. Always we have a choice."

Orion fell silent and smiled to himself. He had finally found his words. He breathed a sigh of relief and, with a determined look in his eyes, he added: "Yes, the eighteenth goal concerns the development of the being itself.

"Each being must turn its awareness to its own inner world. There, the being must understand and practice accepting what it encounters. And when life's path presents choices, in which the being's weakness or strength can govern the outcome, it must practice choosing the strengths. Let the good develop. Thus it will become part of the positive development of the outer world. And thus the seventeen goals will be fully attained."

Orion thought for another moment, and something inside him came to expression. "Because the good," he said, "the good that resides in us, and that we may desire to achieve for our own benefit, always turns out also to benefit others than ourselves in the end. It turns out to benefit that and those around us even more, the whole."

"As we work on reaching the eighteenth goal by transforming our inner weaknesses into their opposite strengths, we must also realise the truth that resides in the goal. The truth that brightly radiates this: We can only create and maintain equality, freedom, and love on the luminous planet when we practice acting as if, exploring how, and finally realising that *we are one*."

38

Orion sat on a flowering blanket near the planet's luminous centre. Surrounding him were bright green plants growing towards the light in the sky. He tried to comprehend the feeling that at this moment filled most of his being; he felt as if he had been travelling and had finally reached his destination. He was happy to have arrived but at the same time also felt full of the long journey. A feeling that contained both joy and understanding. An understanding of the birth of joy. Orion smiled and let his light merge with the air around him.

"Orion, dear heavenly shepherd, dear truth hunter," a voice suddenly called behind him. It was Parshi, who stood in The Final Place, waving. Orion laughed and waved back. Then he noticed the planet's other beings, who approached Parshi in a group. Chunlian went in front. Orion thought that she radiated the wisdom of a strong beginning that carried the now into a brighter future. Just after her followed two groups naturally. In one walked Havar, Raven, and Pea with good, steady strides. In the second group, where cheerful voices drifted like a lively breeze between them, walked Lima, Matu, Sahar, Ino, Nuki, Terra, and Tahi. Behind them went Wirtsch, a wide smile on her face. She looked back at Pheko, Bhoukh, Agua, and Odimma, who moved so gracefully that it looked as if they were carried forward by an invisible string connected to the many beings in front of them.

When all the beings of the luminous planet arrived at The Final Place, Orion saw that they were all looking at Chunlian. She held a stone in her small hands and gave Orion a look full of love. He stood up and walked towards all the assembled beings.

The stone was placed among the other seventeen coloured stones at The Final Place. It filled the important gap that had been in the circle until now. When the light of the fire shone on the new stone, Orion could fully appreciate its magical colour that glowed with greatness; a clear, deep purple that shone on Orion like a bright star. He shone back.

The planet's seventeen beings, who had taken position in front of each of their stones, looked expectantly at Orion. Calmly but purposefully, he moved closer. Now he stood behind the purple stone and felt his heart beating in his chest. Orion smiled gratefully at the many loving eyes around him. Then he took a deep breath and walked the final step into the space in front of the eighteenth stone. A physical silence lived, for no physical words could describe this moment. But on an inner plane, it was anything but silent. In the bright light of the fire, the planet's souls raised their arms and took each other's hands. In a great flash, everything went white. The fire emitted the most incredible bursts of flame, giving

179

out so much warmth and light that it was more than the eye could bear to see. As a lively wind, the brightness of the flames spread among the eighteen beings, and they were all filled with the same inexplicable feeling.

In this moment, they were all connected. Would forever be so. All the life that filled their past, existed in their presence, and would create their future, was forged into one. They became a whole.

The planet radiated such warmth that it generously delighted the developing existences of its admirers. Somewhere in the universe it flourished and shone wiser day by day. It radiated a love in the purest light that shone so genuinely that anyone was immediately drawn closer to themselves. Simply at the sight of it. On closer examination, it was discovered that a tale of a search for truth lay behind the planet's wonderful radiance. A tale of an inner light that completed the luminous planet.